A WITCH FOR MR. WINTER

WITCHES OF CHRISTMAS GROVE, BOOK 3

DEANNA CHASE

ABOUT THIS BOOK

Lily Paddington has a gift, but to her, it's more of a curse. Three years ago, she walked into her husband's dream and found out he'd been lying to her for months. Now she's divorced, and doing whatever she can to make ends meet while raising her son on her own. After being unlucky in love, she has a hard time trusting anyone. But when she finds herself stranded in a small town overnight with Chase Garland, her walls start to crumble.

Chase Garland lost his wife in a traffic car accident over a year ago and has moved to Christmas Grove to start over. He's content with his new job making magical edible chocolates at Love Potions, and even though he's told himself he'll never love again, there's a charming co-worker he can't seem to stop thinking about. After a night in a remote skiing town, it's time for him to make a choice: allow himself to open his heart or give in to the fear of losing in love again.

CHAPTER ONE

$\mathcal{L}$ ily Paddington could still feel her toes tingling. The kiss she'd shared with the man sitting across from her had rocked her world. One minute she'd been telling herself that getting involved with him was a bad idea and the next, she'd let a sprig of mistletoe get in the way of her resolve. Now it was a half hour later, and she couldn't stop thinking about his warm lips claiming hers.

"Lily?" Chase Garland asked, pulling her out of her haze.

"Huh?"

He nodded toward the waitress. "Are you ready to order?"

"Oh, right. Yes," she stammered. "Um, I'll have the seared salmon with lemon risotto."

"One of my favorites," the waitress said. "We have an excellent sauvignon blanc that the chef recommends to pair with this dish. Would you like me to bring you a glass?"

"I don't usually drink much," Lily said then shook her head. "You know what? It's a night off. Why not?"

Chase grinned at her and then turned to the waitress. "I'll have the same. Why don't you bring us the bottle?"

"My pleasure." She jotted it down before rushing off to put their order in.

Lily took a sip of her water, feeling awkward. Everything about the situation felt like a date. Like a twenty-four-hour getaway for two lovers to steal a little time together. Only they weren't together at all. She and Chase were friends and coworkers. The kiss had only happened because of a silly mistletoe tradition.

Earlier that day, the espresso machine at Love Potions had given up the ghost, and because it took too long to ship, Chase had offered to run up to South Lake Tahoe to get the only one they could find within a few hours' drive. He'd then asked Lily to accompany him to help him select some Christmas presents for his nieces. She'd agreed since they'd planned to be back early in the evening. Then Chase's SUV had broken down in Wonderland, the small ski town halfway between Christmas Grove and South Lake Tahoe. They'd been stuck with no way to get back, no one to pick them up, and a hotel room with only one bed.

One bed.

Alone with the man she'd had a crush on for a year.

Lily's entire body flushed as she gazed at him, her mind going places it shouldn't. What would be the harm in spending the night in his arms? She was single. He was single. Her friend Ilsa was taking care of her son. Lily had twenty-four hours away from her real life. Why couldn't she enjoy herself a little?

Oh, right. That coworker thing could be an issue. If she didn't have to see Chase five days a week, maybe she could let her guard down and... do what? Throw herself at him? She swallowed a bark of laughter. Lily hadn't been with anyone since she'd kicked her ex to the curb. She was fairly certain that any seduction attempts on her end would be comical at best and cringeworthy at worst.

"So, Lily," Chase said, leaning forward as he spoke. "You told me before that you aren't interested in dating, but you didn't really tell me why. Is it me, or are you just not interested in dating at all?"

She choked on her sip of water and sputtered, "What?"

Chase grinned, obviously enjoying making her flustered. "I was just sitting here thinking how much I'm enjoying being here with you and was wondering why you aren't interested in dating."

Her cheeks burned, and Lily hated that she was acting like a preteen who'd never had a boy pay attention to her before. But the truth was, she had very little experience with men. She'd had one boyfriend in high school who'd been more like a best friend, and then in her first year of college she'd met her ex-husband. A year later, she'd dropped out of college to marry him and follow him across the country.

Lily cleared her throat. "I have my son Evan to think about. The divorce was hard on him. I don't want him getting attached to someone who won't be a permanent fixture in his life."

Chase nodded. "Understandable." He gazed at her, and his brow furrowed as if he were trying to figure her out.

"What?" she asked.

He shook his head. "Never mind. It's really none of my business."

The waitress appeared with their wine. After uncorking it, she poured a taste into a glass and offered it to Lily.

Lily took a sip. The crisp white wine had a hint of citrus. She smiled up at the waitress and nodded. "It's good."

The waitress smiled and filled both of their glasses.

Once she was gone, Lily clutched her glass and stared at Chase as he tasted the wine. "What isn't any of your business? We're friends, right? If you want to ask me something, then go ahead and ask."

Chase placed his glass back on the table. His green eyes were full of interest when he gave her a nod and said, "All right. You already know I'd like to take you out, so I don't want you thinking I'm pressuring you. I completely understand not wanting to involve Evan in anything casual, but I'm just really curious why you don't want to pursue anything serious. After getting to know you this past year, you seem to really value family."

Lily's heart squeezed painfully. As a young girl, she'd only had her mom. Then when her mom passed away the summer before Lily started college, the only thing she'd wanted was to start a family. It was why she'd been willing to interrupt her education to marry Sean. Then he'd blown up the life they'd built and left her with nothing but her son. She met Chase's gaze head on. "I had a family once. It didn't work out. And honestly, Chase, I have thought about dating again, but the one time I went on a date, it was a disaster. I just decided that for now, it's not really in the cards for me. It's better for Evan if I just focus on the two of us."

His warm gaze was full of understanding as he nodded. "I get it. Really. It took me a long time after I lost my wife to decide I was ready to try again." He reached over and squeezed her hand. "Can I ask a favor?"

"What kind of favor?"

"I'd like to fix that date memory for you. Show you that not all dates are awful."

Lily stiffened her spine. "Chase, I already told you that—"

He raised a hand in acknowledgment. "I know. You're not

up for dating. I heard you. I just want to take you out tonight, as friends, so when or if you're ready, you know what a good date looks like."

She narrowed her eyes at him, half amused and half exasperated. "You think highly of your dating skills." She glanced around at the restaurant. "We're having dinner together. Doesn't this already qualify as a date? As friends of course."

"Only if the date doesn't end right after dinner," he said with a glint in his eyes.

Chuckling, Lily shook her head. "Do you honestly think there's anything to do in Wonderland after seven o'clock on a weeknight?"

"Yes. I do." He winked and then picked up his glass and took another sip of wine.

"I very much doubt it, but I can't wait to see what you have planned."

"It's a yes then?" he asked.

Lily wasn't sure why she was agreeing to his request for a date. Maybe it was the fact that they were stuck in a small town away from real life, but she had to admit that she didn't even consider saying no. Even if all they did was take a walk down Main Street and grab an after-dinner coffee, it would be better than the disaster date she'd had a few months ago. The one she'd walked out on before the waiter had even brought the check. She deserved one night of fun. Right?

Of course she did.

"It's a yes. But only as friends," she confirmed.

"Only as friends." He grinned at her. Then after a moment, he sobered. "I think I'm relieved there's no pressure, since this is the first date I've been on since I lost my wife."

Lily put the piece of bread down that she'd been buttering

5

and gave him her full attention. "You rarely talk about her." She winced, wondering why she'd stated the obvious. "I'm sorry. You don't have to say anything."

"It's okay." He gave her a sad smile. "You're right; I don't. It was sudden, a car accident."

"That's devastating," she said, and this time she reached out to squeeze his hand.

Chase wrapped his fingers around hers as he nodded. "It was. But as a friend told me recently, it's time to start living again." He pasted a bright smile on. "And that's what I intend to do. So, friend, how do you feel about snowshoeing under the stars?"

"Snowshoeing?" she sputtered. "Are you serious?"

"Yep." He pulled a flier out of his pocket and handed it to her.

Lily glanced at it and smiled when she spotted a drawing of an elf holding a sign that read, *Let us guide you to the north star, but tip well since we'll be out of work come January.* It had prices, times, and an address. No reservations necessary. "It looks fun, but I'm not sure I'm dressed for it."

His gaze roamed over her, making a tingle run up her spine. "Have you ever been snowshoeing before?"

She shook her head, unable to speak for fear she'd tell him to skip the stroll in the snow and just take her back to the inn. He had to stop looking at her like that, or she was going to lose all of her resolve and beg him to forget everything she'd said about just being friends.

"Don't worry. Your jeans and sweater are fine. As long as you don't fall into the snow, you'll stay dry."

"And if I do fall, then what?" she asked.

"Then we'll strip you out of them when we get back to the inn," he said. To her surprise, his cheeks flushed red and he hastily added, "I didn't mean we. I meant you. You'd get out of your wet clothes."

Lily desperately wanted to ask *what if I want your help*, but she bit her tongue and kept her flirty words to herself. She'd said friends. Just friends. And that's what they were going to be.

Then why was the little voice in the back of her head telling her that she was making a huge mistake? Chase Garland was a catch, and any woman would be lucky to have him.

Lily shrugged off the thought and said, "Snowshoeing on a first date certainly is original. I'm looking forward to it."

He raised one eyebrow. "First date?"

She flushed again. "As friends."

He nodded and held up his wine glass. "As friends."

She clinked her glass to his and could already tell she was in way over her head. No matter what she told herself, she'd never think of Chase Garland as just a friend.

CHAPTER TWO

*C*hase Garland couldn't stop staring at Lily. He'd always found her attractive, but this was the only time he'd ever spent time with her alone outside of work. It was also the first time he'd let himself acknowledge there was something magical about her. She had an innocence about her that drew him in, but was also tough as nails when she needed to be. He was a sucker for that combination of softness and strength.

"Do I have lettuce in my teeth or something?" she asked, covering her mouth with her hand. They were standing outside the restaurant, waiting for a local ride share to pick them up and take them to the snowshoeing trail.

He laughed. "No. It's not a crime to admire a beautiful woman, is it?"

Lily rolled her eyes. "Please. My hair is a mess, the little makeup I put on this morning has to be long gone now, and my jeans have a hot cocoa stain on my left thigh."

"Is that why you smell like a Kiss Me Chocolate Love

Potion?" he asked, smirking at her. "You know you didn't need a potion to get me to kiss you. All we needed was mistletoe."

"Stop," she said with a laugh and pressed her hand to his forearm. "You know I don't mess with Mrs. Pottson's potions."

Chase covered her hand with his and laughed with her. When he sobered, he added, "You know there's nothing wrong with a little magic every now and then."

Lily shrugged one shoulder. "I'm not so sure about that."

He raised both eyebrows. "There's a story there."

"You could say that." She was debating whether she wanted to tell him her story when a horse-drawn sleigh rounded the corner and pulled to a stop in front of them.

A shorter-than-average person dressed in an elf costume jumped down and bowed low with a flourish. "Your chariot has arrived."

Lily glanced at Chase. "You ordered us a sleigh to take us to the trail?"

He glanced at his phone and then at the elf. "You're from Joyful Rides?"

"Yes, sir. We run until the snow melts." He produced a wooden step stool, seemingly out of nowhere, and grabbed Lily's hand to help her up into the sleigh.

"Thank you," she said and settled onto the leather seat.

Chase followed, and once he was seated, the elf snapped his fingers, making a fuzzy blanket appear on Lily's lap.

"Wow. Full-service treatment," Lily said, happily tucking the blanket around them.

"Enjoy your ride," the elf said with a tip of his pointy hat.

The elf vanished, and the sleigh jerked forward as the bells attached to the sides of the sleigh started to play a classical version of "Winter Wonderland."

Lily let out a delighted laugh. "This was unexpected."

Chase grinned at her. "It's not unlike the magical horseless carriage rides in Keating Hollow."

"True. Have you been on it?" she asked.

He shook his head. "No. Have you?"

"Nope." She glanced away as she added, "Evan always asks to go, but I never have the extra money, so we just walk around town and look at the Christmas decorations."

Chase paused, taking in the fact that her money was so tight that she couldn't splurge on a carriage ride. He knew raising a child on her own was tough, but he hadn't stopped to consider just *how* tough it might be. "Carriage rides are nice and all, but they don't beat a sleigh ride. Especially one in a charming ski town while on a date."

She eyed him and her lips twitched with humor as she added, "A friends-only date."

"Sure. Friends. It's still romantic as hell though, right?" There was no denying that fact.

"It would be better if it was snowing," she said and sat back in her seat.

Chase glanced around at the clear night. "Maybe there's a chance we'll get some flurries later."

She laughed. "Not likely."

"Well, with a little magic, one should never rule it out," he said, imagining a light snowfall at the end of the night. In a perfect world, he'd brush a snowflake off her cheek and kiss her goodnight. But since she was insisting on friends only, he'd respect her boundaries and shift into friend mode.

"If you say so," she said, sounding skeptical.

As the horse trotted along, pulling the sleigh down a wooded street, he studied her. "What is it that bothers you about magic?"

"What do you mean?" she asked. But when she glanced

away again, he recognized her tell that she wasn't all that comfortable with the direction of their conversation.

Curious, Chase pressed on. "Earlier you implied that magic wasn't really something you cared for, and just now you dismissed my comment about magic maybe giving us some snow flurries this evening. Are you against it?" He gestured to the sleigh that was obviously enchanted, considering there was no driver and the bells were playing actual songs instead of just jingling with the motion of the sleigh. "Does this make you uncomfortable? We can always call a cab or something."

"Oh, no," she said, looking up at him. "The sleigh is great. Stuff like this is fine, enchanting even. It's just that other things, like love potions and unusual powers that might not be very ethical, bother me."

He nodded slowly, trying to understand what she was trying to say. "You mean you don't like it when someone is given a love potion without consent or maybe someone uses their power to manipulate a person or situation for their own gain."

"Yes. Exactly. Or when someone's privacy is invaded," she added.

"Care to elaborate?" he asked.

"On what?"

"How someone uses their magic to invade someone's privacy?" Chase couldn't help but be intrigued by her. She kept a lot close to the vest, and Chase really wanted her to let him in.

Lily sucked in a breath and let it out slowly. "You know how people say don't ask questions you don't want the answers to?"

He chuckled. "Is that your way of telling me to mind my own business?"

She gave him a shy smile. "No. I'm trying to explain."

"Sure. I'm listening."

The sleigh made a right turn onto a road that was lined with elaborately decorated Christmas trees and had a large herd of reindeer watching as they slid along the snow.

"Do you have a magical gift?" she asked him.

"Other than my ability to make the perfect truffle?" he asked with a smirk.

"How modest of you," she said with a smirk of her own. "Yes, other than that."

He shook his head. "No. Not that I'm aware of."

"I didn't think I did either for a long time," Lily blurted. "But after I had Evan, this thing started happening with my ex, Sean. I'd have questions, wondering if he was always truthful. Then the next thing I knew, I was dreamwalking into his private dreams."

"Dreamwalking, huh?" Chase asked. "That's sort of fascinating."

"No. No it isn't," Lily insisted. "Do you have any idea what it's like to walk into your spouse's dream and then learn they are having an affair?"

"Ouch." Chase's heart ached for her, and a surge of white-hot anger filled his gut. How could anyone betray her that way?

"Yeah. Ouch," she agreed. "At first, I wanted to believe that what I saw was just a dream, but I recognized the woman. She worked in his office. After the third time of seeing them together in his dreams, I finally went down to the office. It only took twenty minutes until I saw them walk out together for lunch. He was holding her hand and then..." She trailed off, shaking her head. "It doesn't matter what happened next. Only that they were definitely having an affair."

"I'm so sorry, Lily," Chase said, taking her hand in both of his. "That must've been awful."

Her eyes glistened in the moonlight as she nodded. But when she spoke, instead of sadness there was venom in her tone. "It was. The divorce was messy, and Sean fought me through a horrific custody battle. In the end, he got what he wanted, joint custody, and then never once exercised that right. He moved Back East with his girlfriend and hasn't seen Evan in over three years."

"What a jackass," Chase said, hating that she went through all that.

"He's a selfish bastard," Lily said with a shrug. "It's over now, though, and I haven't heard from him in a long time. While I hate that Evan doesn't understand why his father abandoned him, if he's going to be that terrible of a parent, then it's just better if he stays away."

"I agree." Chase hoped that Sean never showed his face again, because if they crossed paths, Chase was worried he'd deck the guy.

"Anyway," Lily said with a sigh. "That's why I don't think all magic is ethical. I shouldn't have been dreamwalking. People are entitled to their privacy. I shouldn't be able to just walk right into their minds and witness their thoughts, even if they are just dreams."

"But if you didn't, you might never have known about his... ah, extracurricular activities," Chase reasoned, surprised that she seemed to be experiencing guilt when her ex was obviously a complete douchecanoe. "Besides, it doesn't sound like you did it on purpose."

She glanced down at her hands in her lap, and in a quiet voice she said, "I don't think I tried to stop it." When she raised her head and met his gaze, she added, "I wanted to know what was going on. But that wasn't the way to do it. How would you feel if I just walked into your dreams? If it were me, I'd feel exposed and probably violated somehow."

Chase couldn't help himself. She looked so vulnerable right then that he had to reach out and cup her cheek. Give her some sort of comfort. "Dreams aren't the same as reading someone's thoughts. You know that. But even if you were an empath and could hear what people were thinking, as long as you weren't doing it intentionally, then it wouldn't be your fault. As for the dreamwalking, it sounds to me like it's something that just happened. I don't think you should beat yourself up about it. Especially when it comes to your ex. He betrayed you first."

Her expression turned from troubled to one of interest, as if what he'd said resonated. Then she narrowed her eyes and asked, "What if I stepped into your dreams? How would you feel about it?"

His lips tugged into a slow smile. "What kind of dream are we talking about here?"

Her eyes crinkled with amusement. "You're a giant flirt. You know that, right?"

The interesting thing about her observation was that Chase hadn't flirted with anyone in a very long time. Not since before his wife passed. He'd been in a dark place, and it had taken months to find the light again. "It's fun though, right?"

"Yes. It is," she admitted. The moonlight illuminated her soft features, and Chase had to glance away for fear he'd cross her friendship boundaries and kiss her again.

The sleigh finally came to a stop next to a small shack that was covered in holiday lights. There was a bench and a large sign that read, *Welcome, Chase and Lily. Strap your snowshoes on and get ready for a romantic moonlit stroll.*

CHAPTER THREE

*L*ily gaped at the sign then at Chase. "Did you set this up?"

He blinked and slowly shook his head. "No. I called to make sure we could rent the snowshoes, but I didn't even tell them our names."

"Well, someone must have." Lily climbed out of the sleigh, with Chase right behind her. As soon as they were on solid ground, the sleigh and it's horse glittered with gold light and then vanished into thin air.

"Whoa," Lily said, staring at the space with widened eyes.

"This town really is something else," Chase said.

"You can say that again. I hope you have cell reception for when we need a ride back."

"I do," he confirmed, looking at his phone.

She nodded and walked over to the shack. Just before she got there, she swore she saw a flash of green velvet disappear into the line of trees behind it. She peered into the structure, finding only snowshoes lined up against the wall with no one manning the booth. There was a sign that indicated they should leave the rental fee in the lockbox and to return the snowshoes when they were done.

"Did you see that?" Chase asked, nodding toward the tree line.

"I saw a flash of green velvet. Do you think there's some elf circle trying to play matchmaker?" she asked with a laugh.

"Possibly." He grinned at her. "That would make the most sense, since one was manning the sleigh when it came to pick us up."

Lily shook her head. "This town is even quirkier than Christmas Grove."

"I don't think that's necessarily a bad thing. Do you?"

"No, it's not." Lily watched him as he selected a pair of snowshoes for both of them. There was a small smile on her lips, and she realized that, despite unloading all her baggage on him during the ride over and the stress of the car breaking down in a strange town, she was having more fun than she'd had in years. Chase Garland was the kind of man that just put her at ease. He was happy to take life as it came and make the most of it. At least he was this night, and that wasn't something she was used to.

When she'd been married to Sean, she had always been on edge. He didn't deal well when things didn't go according to plan. If this had happened to them, she imagined he'd have spent all evening calling around until he found someone, anyone, to get them back home. And if that didn't work, he'd spend the rest of the night pacing their hotel room, ranting about how everyone else was incompetent and didn't realize how it important it was that he was in the office first thing in the morning.

Lily wouldn't even have tried to point out that someone at his office could cover for him. That business wouldn't cease to happen just because one junior advertising agent would miss a staff meeting. It frustrated her that she hadn't seen the warning signs earlier in their relationship and that it had taken finding out he was cheating for her to leave him.

"Here you go," Chase said, handing her a pair of snowshoes. "Take a seat on the bench over there, and I'll strap your feet in."

Lily's first inclination was to refuse his help. She'd been proving to herself that she didn't need anyone to take care of her for so long now that it was second nature. But as soon as she opened her mouth, she shut it and walked over to the bench. Why did she keep needing to prove her capability? She'd done that over and over again. Maybe just for tonight she could let someone else care for her.

Chase quickly buckled her feet into the snowshoes and then took a seat next to her to strap his own on. When he was done, he stood and took careful strides as he walked back over to the shack and retrieved some hiking poles for both of them. He offered a set to Lily and said, "Here, these will help you keep your balance."

"Thanks." She pushed herself to her feet. "Anything special I should know?"

"Not really. It's just like hiking, only make sure you have a wider stance so you won't step on the inside of your snowshoes." He demonstrated by moving one foot a little sideways before he started to walk slowly down the path.

Lily nodded, lifted her foot, and promptly got it caught on her hiking pole. She let out a small cry as she fell face-first into the snow.

"Oh, no. Lily, are you all right?" Chase asked.

She rolled over to find him moving quickly toward her, his expression worried.

"Did you hurt anything?" He crouched down and brushed a wet lock of hair out of her eyes.

"Just my ego." She gave him a weak smile. "Do you think you can help me up?"

"Of course." He took her poles from her, placed them against the shack with his own, and then grabbed both of her hands and hauled her to her feet. "There you go."

"Thanks." She reached for her poles. "Other than my nose stinging from the faceplant, I think I'm good."

Chase cupped her face again, running his thumb over her cheek. "It looks like you'll be okay to me. I can kiss it and make it better if you like."

"There's that flirting again," she said, her lips twitching.

"Want me to stop?"

"No." She soaked up his attention like a love-starved kitten. And since she was already crossing her self-imposed boundaries, she tapped her nose lightly. "I think a kiss is just what my nose needs."

His green eyes glinted and without hesitation, he dropped a soft kiss on her nose.

Lily stood there, wishing she had a reason to kiss him again. More mistletoe would've come in handy at that moment. *Just kiss him, already*, she scolded herself. *It's what you want.* Still, she refrained. It wasn't fair to him for her to be yoyoing back and forth between wanting him and pushing him away. Some harmless flirting was one thing. Kissing him and leading him on was quite another.

"Better?" he asked.

"Yes." She just stood still, content to stare at his handsome face.

Finally, he raised his eyebrows and jerked his head toward the trail. "Want to try that again?"

Lily glanced at the snowy trail with the moon lighting the way along the edge of the trees. "Right. Let's go."

Chase moved to one side and gestured for her to go first.

No doubt he was waiting to see if he'd need to rescue her from the snow again. However, this time she managed to stay upright, and after a few feet, she glanced over at him with a triumphant smile. "This isn't so hard, especially if you don't trip over the poles."

"That does make it easier," he said with a laugh and fell into step alongside her.

Lily glanced over at him and couldn't help asking, "Is this what you were like when you were married?"

His brow was furrowed when he glanced at her. "What do you mean? Did I take my wife on snowshoeing dates?"

"Yeah," she said with a nod and then shook her head. "I mean no, not snowshoeing in particular. I mean were you this easygoing and patient, especially when things didn't go as planned?"

Chase took his time before answering. When he did, he let out a soft, self-deprecating chuckle. "Honestly, probably not."

"No?" Lily found that surprising. "Why not?"

"I think I used to be easygoing in the earlier years. But as time wore on, Heather became more and more critical of my choices. I imagine that if this had happened to us, she would've blamed me for the car breaking down. After she calmed down, she would've gone to dinner with me but then would have demanded we go back to the room while she worked on her computer and I did my best not to disturb her."

"That sounds... stressful," Lily said, unable to imagine treating such a lovely man in such a manner. "What did she do on the computer?"

"She was a tastemaker, ran a blog, and marketed herself as

cool and trendy. From there she had a bunch of clients that had her run their social media. Her image was really important to her. If anything ever went wrong, it was a major disaster. Like the time I was late picking up some dress from a designer that she was supposed to wear to an industry party. They left before I could get there, so she had to wear something else." His tone turned bitter when he added, "She didn't speak to me for days."

Lily was speechless. "All of that over a dress?"

He shrugged. "Apparently the designer was an important up-and-coming player in the fashion industry, and I somehow ruined Heather's chances of being hired as a social media consultant because I made her look like she didn't value the client enough to even show up on time to borrow the garment. The thing is, I told Heather I had a catered event that day and I didn't know if I would make it by five. She dismissed my warning and said she knew I'd make it because I always did."

"I hate to say it, Chase," Lily said gently, not wanting to speak ill of his late wife, but also wanting to make sure he felt supported. "But it sounds like she might've taken you for granted."

"Maybe."

Definitely, she thought. "Every marriage has issues, even the good ones," Lily said, trying to salvage the direction of their conversation. "I'm sure she was just stressed. It couldn't have been easy running that kind of business."

"The real issue was that she found that celebrity-like lifestyle important, while for me it was a lot of stuff that I just didn't care about at all." Chase shook his head. "I hated getting dressed up in a tux and going to ultra-fancy parties where everyone was trying to find investors for their startups or celebrities to market their goods. It was all really superficial.

Meanwhile, I was getting up at the crack of dawn to run my own chocolate shop. Heather never hesitated to boast about that. She loved showing off her business-owner husband but hated it when I put my work over her social obligations to her clients."

Lily paused and pressed her hand against a nearby tree. "It must've been hard when you both had different priorities."

"It was." He waved a hand around at their surroundings. "This is my idea of a good time. Not endless parties with champagne and VIP tickets." Chase sighed. "I don't mean to make it sound like my marriage was horrible. It wasn't. But for the last few years, we didn't exactly see eye to eye."

"I'm sorry," Lily said, meaning it. She knew what it was like to be in a marriage that wasn't working out the way she'd hoped.

"Me, too."

There was silence between them until Lily smiled at him and said, "I wouldn't mind going to a VIP party just once to experience it, but otherwise, I also am drawn to the outdoors. It's why I moved to Christmas Grove. I used to visit the Christmas Tree farm with my grandparents when I was little. I always loved it there. I figured it would be a good place for Evan, too."

"At least you knew where you were moving to when you relocated," Chase said with a laugh. "I chose it based on the job at Love Potions. It was a huge plus that it was near the National Forest."

"You'd never been there before?" she asked, astonished.

"Nope. But when I saw the job opening listed online, I spent a lot of time googling. I knew the moment I saw the pictures of downtown that I would take the job if Mrs. Pottson offered it to me."

"Lucky for us," Lily said even as her cheeks warmed in the cold.

"I'd say I'm the lucky one," he said softly. "I couldn't have asked for a better boss or coworkers."

The sincere look on his face made butterflies flutter in her stomach. She pressed a hand to her abdomen, willing the sensation to go away. She already liked him too much. Getting moon-eyed over him was a really bad idea. Or was it? Lily was having trouble remembering why she decided she shouldn't date him.

"Come on. Let's find out what's at the end of this trail," Chase said.

Lily nodded and hoped the trail was a long one, because she didn't want their date to end.

CHAPTER FOUR

*C*hase hadn't been so comfortable on a date maybe ever. Maybe it was because they'd designated it as a friend date and there wasn't any pressure for more than that. But he didn't think that was the only reason. Lily Paddington was everything he wanted in a partner. Sweet, down-to-earth, open, and easy to talk to. Plus, he admired that she put her son first, no matter what.

His own mother had been driven by her career, just like Heather had. Chase's own childhood had been lonely as he spent countless hours waiting for his parents to come home. Both had worked late nights and weekends to pay for their house in the best neighborhood and their vacation home on the lake. He'd been given the best of everything, but all he really wanted was his parents' attention.

His childhood was why he'd been reluctant to start a family with Heather. It wasn't because he expected her to give up her career. Hell, if it came to that, he'd have been willing to be the stay-at-home dad. He just hadn't been able to stomach the fact that he knew his wife would always be working late and weekends due to her drive to be the best in the business. He wanted a family, the full unit, not one where one parent was so busy that they were never around. And that's what he would've gotten with Heather.

Chase had known Lily for over a year now. He couldn't imagine her sacrificing her time with her son if she didn't absolutely have to. As it was, when she worked extra jobs like at the Christmas tree farm, she often brought Evan with her.

"Why are you staring at me?" Lily asked in a teasing tone.

"I'm admiring your form," he quipped.

Lily laughed. "Sure you are. Should I demonstrate the art of falling again? You could take notes."

"No way. You've gained expert snowshoeing skills since then. Look at how you're wielding those poles. Absolute perfection."

Lily snorted. "You're a charmer, aren't you?"

"I try."

They rounded a cluster of trees and ended in a clearing that was lit up with twinkle lights. About a dozen snowmen in various states of creation dotted the field. Off to the side was another sign that read, *Snowman Field. Make your perfect snowman and enter to win the annual snowman contest.*

"I wonder what the winner of the snowman contest wins," Lily said.

Lightening bugs appeared out of thin air and gathered into a formation that read, *$10,000.*

"Wow, that's impressive," Chase said.

Lily's pulse sped up. Was this real? "How does one enter?"

The lightening bugs formed again, this time into an arrow that pointed toward a board near the sign. Lily released her feet from her snowshoes and hurried over to the sign. There were signup sheets and envelopes. She turned around and grinned at Chase. "You know we're doing this, right?"

"I wouldn't dream of skipping it," he said and freed his feet from his snowshoes.

Lily took off into the clearing and found a section that was big enough for them to form their snowman. Without waiting for Chase, she started packing together the snow to build the base of her snowman. She was so into it that she didn't even notice when Chase arrived and crouched down next to her.

"Your hands are going to freeze if you keep that up," Chase said.

She startled at the sound of his voice and jerked her head up to find him holding out a pair of mittens for her. "You're like a minor miracle. Where did you get these?"

"There's a lost and found box over there. If you look at them a little more carefully, you'll notice they don't match." He nodded to her hands. "Hold them out for me."

Lily did as he asked and waited patiently as he tugged the mittens on. "Thank you."

"You're very welcome." He glanced at her mound of snow and raised one eyebrow. "Your snowperson seems to have lumpy junk in his or her trunk."

Lily scoffed. "Are you disparaging my snowperson building skills?"

"Maybe a little." He chuckled and started to pat down the lumpy areas on her snowman.

"You really think that's going to help?" Lily asked as she dug her mittened hands into a fresh pile of snow.

Chase chuckled. "I guarantee it will look better when I'm done." He kept his attention on his work as he continued, "You're looking at the 2005 champion of the annual snow—oomph!" A ball of snow hit him in the shoulder, knocking him just off balance enough that he fell onto his butt. He stared at her with his mouth open.

Lily giggled and then threw her second ball of snow. It landed with a thud right in the middle of his chest.

"Oh, it's on, Lily Paddington," he said with a playful growl and then unleashed his own assault of snowballs.

Lily cried out and scrambled away from him, trying to dodge the onslaught of his attack. But she was no match for Chase. He not only pegged her in the back and shoulder, he caught up with her far too easily and tackled her into the snow. "No!" she cried, laughing as he tried to pin her arms over her head. "Stop! We have work to do."

"You started this," he said with laughter lacing his tone. "Now I'm going to finish it."

He let go with one of his hands while trying to pin both wrists with the other one.

Lily used that opportunity to grab a handful of snow and smash it into his face. She was laughing so hard at his reaction that she couldn't fight him off and ended up on her back again, with his body pinning her.

"You think you're funny, don't you?" he said playfully, holding a handful of snow right over her face.

Laughter continued to bubble up as she shook her head and forced out a breathless, "No."

"You're a terrible liar," he said in a low, gruff voice. And then before she could answer, he pressed the snow to her forehead and rubbed it down her face.

Lily let out a shriek of surprise and bucked up, trying to dislodge him, but he was far too heavy.

"I told you I was going to finish this," he said, staring down at her.

Lily stilled as the laughter faded. Suddenly their playing

was all too real. He was lying on top of her, the weight of him pressing into her. And his face was so close. All she had to do was lift her head a few inches, and his lips would be hers again. Her tongue darted out, and she watched as his eyes tracked the movement.

"Chase?" she whispered breathlessly, ready to let go of all her hesitations. She wanted him and could think of nothing more romantic than making out with him in the clearing, underneath the stars, in the middle of a bunch of snowmen.

He abruptly let her go and rolled off her. "Sorry. That was... I shouldn't have been holding you down like that."

Lily sat up, suddenly cold from rolling around in the snow. She wrapped her arms around herself and shivered.

"Damn, now you're half frozen." He shrugged off his jacket and wrapped it around her shoulders.

"You didn't have to do that. I started this snowball war," she said, grinning at him. "And it was so much fun I'd do it again."

"Yeah? You're not upset?"

"Why would I be upset?" she asked.

"I thought I might've taken it too far." He got to his feet and held out a hand to help her up.

Once Lily was standing, she squeezed his hand. "You didn't. If anyone did, it was me. How about we make the most kickass snowman anyone has ever seen and then get back to the room before we freeze our backsides off."

"Kickass, huh? You think you can keep your snowman bodies lump free?"

"There's nothing wrong with a few lumps," she said indignantly.

He let his gaze roam over her body and let out a small chuckle. "You know, you're right. There's absolutely nothing wrong with a couple of lumps. In fact, I'd say sometimes they're just right."

Lily's entire body heated under his gaze. That look was one of a man thinking way dirtier thoughts than one who was planning on finishing a snowman. "Whatever you're thinking, you need to get your mind out of the snow. We have work to do."

"Yes, ma'am," he said, giving her a half-assed salute. "Let's get rolling."

Shaking her head, she reached down and threw one last snowball at him. It was a halfhearted attempt though, and it broke apart before it ever even hit him.

"That's just sad," he teased and leaned in to kiss her on the cheek.

An electric spark traveled from the kiss all the way to the center of her chest. She pressed a hand over her heart as if to capture the feeling and knew in that moment that she'd never be able to resist him.

"Let's get serious," Chase said. "We have ten grand to win." He winked and then went back to smoothing the body of the snowman.

The idea of ten grand was more than enough to get Lily motivated. The pair of them worked in unison, shaping the body of the snowman until he looked like he was growing right out of the blanket of snow on the ground. After that, the head went quickly.

Once the body was done, Lily stood back and studied their creation. "We need good props for his face, something for arms, and definitely some sort of crazy hat. Something to get everyone's attention."

Chase nodded thoughtfully, walked over to the hiking

poles, grabbed a pair, and then carefully added them to the snowman for the arms.

Lily laughed, took off her mittens, and placed them on the ends in order to give him hands.

"Perfect," Chase said. 'Now for the face." He jogged over to the lost and found and started rummaging around.

"I seriously doubt you'll find a corncob pipe in there," Lily said, joining him.

"Let's hope not," he said with a chuckle. Chase hit the jackpot with a scarf and even a fedora.

"Seriously, how did someone leave a fedora behind?" Lily asked.

"They were probably having a snowball fight and lost it in the snow," he said as he crossed the clearing to add their found items.

Lily chuckled, thinking about a man losing his fancy hat. Then she went salvaging to find items to build the face. Twenty minutes later, the snowman had pine needles for a mouth, the tops of pine cones for eyes, and the extra button from Chase's coat as his nose. Lily crossed her arms over her chest as she studied the snowman. "He looks pretty good, but he could really use some personality."

"There's a pink tutu in the lost and found," Chase offered.

"Seriously?" Lily asked, excited about turning her snowperson into a ballerina.

"No." His eyes danced in amusement.

Lily mimed punching him in the arm. "You're the worst."

"You think so?"

"No," she said with a sigh. "What else was in the lost and found?"

"Nothing much."

She pursed her lips together and had an idea. After

rummaging around in her purse, she came up with a small pad of paper and a Sharpie. She scribbled the word *Press* on one of the sheets of paper, tore it off and tucked it into the rim of the fedora. Then she shoved the Sharpie into the side of the snowman's mouth, making it appear he was holding it between his lips, and balanced the notebook in one of the mittens.

"What do you think?" she asked Chase.

"It just needs one more thing." He grinned as he pulled out a camera that was tucked into his pocket. It wasn't just any camera either. It was an older film camera with an adjustable lens, and it had a green velvet strap attached for someone to carry it around their neck. Chase placed it over the snowman's head. "There. Now he's a photo journalist."

Lily let out a whoop of joy and clapped her cold hands together. "He's definitely full of personality."

"If we don't win, it won't be for a lack of doing our best," Chase said and strode over to the sign where he grabbed the paperwork for Lily to fill out. "Put your info here. It was your idea."

"I don't think it was really mine, but that's fine. I'll just put us both down."

"Lily," he argued, "you do not need to include me. I did this just for fun."

She put her hand up, stopping him from speaking. "We do it this way or we don't enter at all. We both had a hand in this, and that's all there is to it."

"Fine." He put his hands up in surrender.

She quickly filled out their information, stuffed the entry into the envelope, and dropped it into a lockbox. "How much you want to guess they take one look at these, throw them all out, and just reward whoever they want to?"

"It's always possible with these things," Chase agreed. "But if they don't honor it, they'll have to deal with the ire of the people of Wonderland, and you know no one wants to go through that."

"Let's hope you're right." Lily searched for her snowshoes but quickly realized they were nowhere to be found. "Uh, Chase?"

"Yeah?" he asked.

"Snowshoes? Where do you think they are?"

He frowned and came to help. Both pairs were just gone. "Well, this is awkward."

She nodded her agreement. "Now what?"

A white horse suddenly shot through the trees and came to a full stop in front of them. He was tall, with a gorgeous mane of white hair that practically shimmered in the moonlight. Lily started to wonder if he was enchanted too.

"He's already saddled," Chase said, moving slowly toward the horse. "Looks like the elves have sent us a gift."

Lily remained skeptical. "This horse must belong to someone."

"Sure. But he's not doing them any good being out here in the cold," Chase argued. "But he will make a handy ride back to town."

"True. And it's getting late," she said.

The horse was perfectly still as Chase helped Lily up into the saddle and then was just as calm when he joined her.

"Ready?" he asked.

Lily wrapped her arms around him from behind and pressed her cheek to his back. "As ready as I'll ever be."

The horse trotted gently back down the path toward where Chase was parked. On the way, the stars seemed to get brighter. Lily had her head tilted up, admiring the crisp clear night when she saw it.

"It's a shooting star," she gasped, pointing in the direction of the light. "Did you see it?"

Chase nodded.

"Make a wish."

"Now?" he asked.

"Yes, now. And make it something good. Make it count," she ordered.

He glanced over his shoulder at her, giving her a smug smile. "You, too. Make it good, *friend.*"

The word friend pissed her off just enough that she had no choice but to make the wish she'd been telling herself was a bad idea all night. But with her hands wrapped around his solid body and the way he'd listened to her and made her laugh, there was no denying what she really wanted.

Lily closed her eyes and wished for...

Chase Garland.

CHAPTER FIVE

The white horse stopped right in front of the cheery, lit-up inn. Chase was sorry to see their date come to an end. He couldn't remember the last time he'd had so much fun. He loved the way Lily had been up for a little adventure while they were stranded. She lived the definition of making the most out of every opportunity, and that's exactly the type of person he wanted in his life.

He jumped down to the sidewalk and held his hand out to her. Lily smiled at him, took his hand and let him help her off the horse. Once they were both on solid ground again, the horse nickered at them once, threw his head back, and trotted down the street. Before he turned the corner, the horse vanished into thin air, leaving the street silent and empty.

Lily smiled. "Wonderland really pulls out all the stops, doesn't it?"

"It seems so," he said, staring down at her, taking in her sparkling eyes and cheerful expression. "Or maybe they were putting on a show just for us."

Lily chuckled. "Oh, yeah? What makes us so special?"

"Not us, you," he said, unable to stop himself from flirting with her.

She flushed pink.

Chase felt his heart flutter. Damn. He was getting in way too deep. It was time to put some distance between them before he lost himself to her. He started to drop her hand, but Lily clutched it, tightening her grip on him.

He glanced down at their connection and then back into her eyes. "Lily?"

She tugged him closer, until they were just a few inches apart. The air was charged between them as she licked her lips.

"This doesn't feel like how friends end a date," he said, his voice husky. The impulse to wrap his arms around her, to bury his hands in her long blond hair, was strong.

"No, it doesn't." Her eyes were fixated on his mouth as her breathing shallowed.

Chase sucked in a breath and forced himself to take a step back. "I don't want to do anything that will cross your boundaries. Maybe we should—"

Lily took a step forward, invading his personal space. Her voice was a whisper as she asked, "What if my boundaries have changed?"

"Oh, damn," Chase said, closing his eyes for just a moment. When he opened them, she was staring up at him with undeniable desire. "I'm not strong enough to resist you."

"Then don't." Lily used her free hand to lightly stroke his jawline.

His mouth went dry, and he wanted more than anything to claim her lips with his, but he had to make sure this was what she really wanted. That she wasn't going to regret their evening together. "Does this mean you've changed your mind about dating?" Gods, did he really just ask that? What was he, fifteen? Just because a woman wanted to get intimate that didn't mean she was in love with him. His ego wasn't that inflated. "I mean, I'm not trying to pressure you. It's just that you said before you can't do casual, so I'm just trying to make sure we're both on the same page here."

She bit down on her bottom lip and looked up at him with apprehension as she said, "Would you mind terribly if it were just for tonight?"

His heart sank. He wanted so much more than she was offering. But at the same time, he knew he'd never be able to say no. "You mean like what happens in Wonderland stays in Wonderland?"

Lily nodded and pressed her hand to her chest. "It's been a very long time since I've been with anyone. I just don't trust easily. But I trust you, and I like you. And we're here in this place, sharing a room." She reached up and caressed his lower lip with her thumb. "I don't want you to think I'm using you. It's just that I really like you, but I don't want to complicate things for Evan."

Use him? Hell, he didn't care about that. Not one bit. His only hesitation was that he didn't know if he could give her up after only one night.

She pulled him closer. "Chase do you think we could have this one night together?"

"Just tonight?" he asked thickly.

"Yes." Lily stared up at him, her gaze focused as she waited for him to reply.

"Tomorrow we go back to being just friends?" The statement was more for himself. He knew exactly what Lily was asking. And why. This was the one rare occasion where she was free of her responsibilities and she could think of only what she wanted.

And what she wanted was Chase.

Lily nodded. "If you're okay with that."

Chase cupped both of her cheeks and held her gaze. "I'm more than okay with that."

The tension in her shoulders eased as she let out a breath. Her eyes fluttered closed as Chase leaned in an claimed her lips with his own. She tasted sweet and perfect and like everything he'd ever dreamed about.

Lily clutched at his shirt with one hand and squeezed his bicep with the other. He wanted her hands everywhere, wanted to thrust his hand into her hair and wrap his arms around her waist, clutching her to him. He just wanted more, all of her. But they were standing in the middle of the street. Lily deserved for him to take his time, to worship her, and to do it away from prying eyes.

Someone cleared their throat as they walked by, pulling Chase out of his lust-filled haze. He pulled back slightly, releasing her, but before she could move too far, he grabbed one of her hands and gently tugged her toward the front door of the inn. "Come on. Let's get you out of the cold."

Lily let out a tinkling laugh. "Funny, I don't feel cold at all."

"You will if I strip you out of your clothes right here," Chase said and opened the door for her.

"That would certainly cause some talk." Lily pumped her eyebrows playfully.

Chase growled. Actually growled. There wasn't anything that turned him on more than a woman who was sexy and playful in the bedroom.

"Oh, gods," she whispered as she visibly shivered.

Chase glanced over at her just as they reached the stairs. "What?"

Her blue eyes had practically turned sapphire. "I was just

thinking about what I've gotten myself into. I don't think I've ever actually been growled at before."

"There's more where that came from." He couldn't stop himself from pulling her into his arms and running a trail of kisses down her neck. Lily tilted her head back and let out a small gasp when he gently bit down at her nape.

"Oh, wow." Lily practically melted in his arms.

He chuckled to himself and then tugged her up the stairs. Chase fumbled with the key outside their door, dropping it at his feet. "Dammit." He reached for it, but Lily beat him to it.

"Here." She slid the key into the door and smiled over her shoulder as she walked inside.

Chase couldn't keep his eyes off her, following as if he was a moth drawn to a flame. He closed and locked the door behind him before joining her next to the bed.

"So…" Lily said, giving him a nervous smile. "We're here."

"We certainly are." Chase gave in to his impulse and buried his hand into her long hair before dropping both hands to her hips and tugging her body until she was flush against him. "I've been dreaming of this ever since you kissed me under the mistletoe."

"Me, too," she said breathlessly.

Holy hell, she was killing him. He wanted her desperately. Wanted to rip her clothes off and ravish her. But the night was still young. Chase vowed to take his time, to worship every inch of her body, and to commit every second to memory. He bent his head, kissing her again, and he let his hands travel underneath her sweater to her soft, smooth skin.

Lily swayed in his arms and then deepened the kiss. One hand caressed the back of his neck, while the other stayed lodged between them just over his heart. She was breathless when she said, "You feel even better than I imagined."

"So do you." Chase's lips found her neck again and he was gratified when she tilted her head, giving him even more access. Her sweater prevented him from going further, and he was just about to make his way back up to her lips when she stepped back, held his gaze, and tugged her sweater over her head. She stood there in the soft lighting, looking absolutely perfect in her red lace bra. His breath caught, and his fingers ached to touch her. But this was her show, and he was going to wait for her next move.

Lily reached out and started working the buttons of his flannel shirt with trembling fingers. Chase stayed still, waiting until she had his shirt open and was pushing it off his shoulders.

Once he was bare, he caught one of her hands and kissed her palm. "Are you all right?"

"I'm perfect," she said, gazing up at him with a vulnerable expression. "You?"

"Desperate for you," he said honestly as he ran his fingers over her collarbone and down to the swell of her breast.

She sucked in a sharp breath and whispered, "Then what are you waiting for?"

It was the signal he needed. Chase didn't waste any time divesting her of the rest of her clothing. He was delighted when she took charge, ridding him of his jeans and then his boxer briefs. She took a tiny step back and swept her gaze over him. He waited for her to get her fill and then ran his hands down her arms, over her ribcage, and back down to her hips.

"You're gorgeous," he said.

"So are you." She placed her hands on his chest, making him shudder with anticipation. And then when she was kissing him again, he was done waiting.

Chase swept her up in his arms and carried her over to the bed.

"This is very caveman of you," she teased.

"Is that a complaint?" he asked.

"Never."

He let out another growl and placed her on the bed. In the next moment, he was moving over her, reveling in the sensation of skin on skin.

Lily smiled up at him. "This is everything I thought it would be."

"You haven't seen anything yet," he assured her and then spent the rest of the night worshipping every inch of her.

CHAPTER SIX

*L*ily's eyes fluttered open and took a moment to adjust in the darkened room. She was snuggled against Chase's chest, her body sore with the delicious ache from their lovemaking. Chase Garland had made her feel like the most beautiful and sensual woman in the world. She'd never felt so good or been so satisfied in her entire life.

The man deserved a freakin' gold medal in not only effort but results.

She couldn't help running her fingers over his muscular pecs. The man must work out when he wasn't at Love Potions, because he had the most gorgeous body she'd ever seen.

Chase stirred under her touch and murmured, "I thought you were asleep."

"I was, but then I woke up next to you, and now I'm wide awake again."

He smiled down at her and tightened his hold on her. "How awake?"

"Very awake." This time Lily covered his body with hers.

"If this is the way you wake me up, feel free to do it

whenever you want," he said, running his fingertips down her spine.

She didn't bother to remind him that this was the only night they'd get. There was no point in spoiling the mood. Instead, she took her time exploring him until finally he growled, something she was beginning to get addicted to, and spun her until she was on her back and he was devouring her again.

～

"YOU'RE DELICIOUS," Lily said, eyeing Chase over her red coffee mug.

"Are you talking to me or your coffee?" Chase asked, giving her that sexy half smile that now made her belly quiver with anticipation.

"You. Although this coffee is possibly the best I've ever had," she said.

His little smile turned into a self-satisfied grin. "Last night was that good, huh?"

Lily rolled her eyes. "Don't go fishing for compliments. You know exactly how much I enjoyed last night."

"Yes. Yes, I do." He winked and took a bite of his toast.

After waking up late and making love one more time, they'd found their way to the Let it Snow diner. The windows were enchanted to make it look as if snow was falling outside while candles were floating over each table, illuminating more light. It was just as enchanting as the rest of the town.

Lily's resolve had vanished. The date they'd had the night before, followed by their lovemaking, had her wondering just exactly how she was going to pretend that she and Chase were just friends. He'd made it clear he wanted to date her, and she was starting to realize that if she bypassed this chance, she might be losing out on what could become something really special.

Her only problem was how to deal with dating him while keeping Evan from getting attached. She put her coffee down on the table and leaned forward. "I know I said that last night was a one-time thing, but how would you feel about us seeing each other occasionally?"

His eyebrows shot up with shock then his eyes flashed with disappointment as he placed his own coffee mug on the table. "You mean like a casual hookup when you find time in your schedule?"

Lily swallowed a groan. Why was she so bad at this? She'd obviously been unclear about her intentions. "No. I'm sorry. That's not what I meant." She buried her face in her hands and rubbed at her tired eyes before meeting his gaze again. "Last night was special. And I'm not even talking about what happened after we got back to the inn."

"You're really trying to wound me, aren't you?" he asked as he mimed stabbing himself in the heart. But his lips twitched in amusement as he added, "My ego is really taking a beating here."

She snorted out a laugh. "Okay, how about this? You were amazing. Your lovemaking skills are unparalleled. They should erect a statue in your honor. Call it Saint—"

"Boner," a lady who was sitting behind Lily interjected. Lily twisted around to find an older woman with white hair, thick glasses, and heavily wrinkled hands beaming at her. "Saint Boner, and it should be in his image, naked like those Greek statues. Only his junk should be erect, so us women have something to pray too."

The woman's breakfast companions all broke out into

giggles. One of them gasped for air and forced out, "Leave it to Francie to verbalize what we're all thinking but are too afraid to say out loud."

Lily stared at them in disbelief until finally a chuckle escaped her lips. "You might be onto something," she said to Francie, who was busy taking a photo of Chase with her iPhone.

"What's your name, dear?" she asked Chase. "I'm going to tag you on Instagram."

Chase cleared his throat. "I don't have an Instagram page."

"Oh, what a shame," Francie said with a pout. "With a magic boner like yours, you'd be Instafamous."

"I don't have a magic boner," he said, his face flushing pink. He gave Lily a pointed look. "Help me out here?"

She threw her head back and laughed. "If you're asking me to deny the magic of your, um... bedroom prowess, you're going to be sadly disappointed. I'm not a very good liar."

All of the older ladies cheered, making such a ruckus that the waitress hurried over to ask what they were celebrating.

"We're cheering for Magic Mike over there and his enchanted penis," Francie said through tears of laughter.

The waitress glanced at Lily and Chase with a confused expression.

Lily put a hand on her arm and said, "They're just teasing. I think their mimosas might have caught up with them."

"Oh, they've just gotten started," the waitress said. Then she lowered her voice and asked, "Are they bothering you? They can get a little wild sometimes."

"Not at all," Lily assured her. "They're fun. Don't worry about a thing."

Chase let out a grunt of disagreement but said nothing. Instead, he downed his coffee and finished off the last piece of his bacon. "I'll go pay, and then we can see when the SUV will be ready."

Lily reached out and grabbed his hand, holding it lightly. "I'm sorry. Can we finish this discussion outside, away from prying grandmas?"

His expression softened and he gave her a nod. "Sure. I'll meet you out there."

When Chase was out of earshot, Lily turned around and said, "You're my type of ladies. I hope I'm lucky enough to be having as much fun as you are when I'm your age."

"Oh, baby. We're the jealous ones," Francie said, nodding toward Chase. "It's not every day a woman finds a sweetheart like that who knows what to do with his package. If I were you, I'd hold on with both hands and never let go." She winked and added, "Take it from me; they're rarer than you think."

Lily didn't doubt her for a moment. She'd already experienced the other side of that coin. "Thanks. I'll take that under advisement." She scooted out of her booth, waved to the women, and went to stand outside.

Chase joined her shortly after.

Lily slipped her arms around his waist, staring up at him. "I'm sorry if that made you uncomfortable."

"Uncomfortable? Why would I be uncomfortable with four women old enough to be my grandmother discussing my sex life?" he asked with a smirk.

"Okay. Noted. I wouldn't care for that either." She stretched up onto her tiptoes and gave him a soft kiss. "What I was trying to say before the Magic Mike groupies interrupted is that I like you. I like you a lot, and despite what I said last night, I was wondering if maybe we could try dating."

He sucked in a soft breath and searched her eyes. "Are you sure that's what you want?"

Lily nodded. "The only issue is that I don't want to involve Evan at this point. He had a rough time adjusting after his father abandoned him, and I really don't want to introduce someone into his life that might not be permanent."

Chase frowned but nodded slowly. "I understand. It's way too soon to involve your son. I wouldn't want to do anything that made you uncomfortable."

Lily let out a relieved breath. "Thank you for that. It means I probably can only see you one night a week when Evan is at his baking class, or if he's staying over with Vin or my dad, which isn't really that often."

"Vin?" he asked.

"Ilsa's stepson. There's a bit of an age difference, but the two of them like to spend time together over at Zach's Christmas tree farm."

"I think I can work with that." He reached out and tucked a lock of her hair behind one ear. They held each other's gazes for a long moment, and then he leaned down and kissed her.

Lily wrapped her arms around him, wishing that they were back at the inn and not standing on the sidewalk in front of the entire town.

"Whoo-hoo! Get it, girl," a familiar female voice called.

"I think Francie approves," Chase muttered.

"Well then, we should do that again." Lily covered his lips with hers and gave the older ladies a show to remember. There were plenty more hoots and hollers as Lily took her time tasting Chase. When she finally broke away, they were both breathless.

"Get a room!" The shout came from someone across the street.

Lily just turned and waved.

The woman pushing a stroller with a toddler who appeared to be passed out scowled at her. "This is a family town."

"How does she know we're not a family?" Chase asked.

Lily snorted. "I bet she and her husband are swingers and that most things are on the table as long as it's behind closed doors."

"Swingers?" he laughed. "That seems like a stretch, don't you think?"

"Oh, Chase. You're so naive," she said, shaking her head. "It's always the ones who protest the loudest who are doing the most in the bedroom."

Shaking his head, he grabbed her hand. "Let's go. We still have an espresso machine to get."

Lily clutched his hand and felt a surge of joy fill her heart. How long had it been since she'd been this happy?

"What are you smiling about?" he asked, eyeing her.

"You, me, this town. It wasn't planned, but you managed to turn it into the best getaway I've ever had."

He stroked her hand with his thumb and said, "You did the same for me. We could always plan another spontaneous car repair. Same time next month?"

Lily laughed and shook her head. "If only, Chase Garland. If only."

CHAPTER SEVEN

$\mathcal{C}$hase tucked his hands into his jacket pockets and dropped his head down against the wind as he strode through the gates of the Frost Family Tree Farm. A storm was rolling in over Christmas Grove, and he planned to hole up in his house for the next few days, but first he needed to pick up a Christmas tree. If he still didn't have one up by Sunday when he Facetimed with his mother, he was certain she'd get on a plane from Vermont to put one up herself. She'd been asking when he was going to decorate ever since Thanksgiving.

He'd been meaning to get a tree, but after the overnight stay in Wonderland with Lily, he'd been distracted and had forgotten all about it. In fact, for the past three days, he'd worked overtime at Love Potions to get caught up on the day he'd missed. It was the worst time of year to take an unexpected day off. But he had to admit he'd do it again in a heartbeat. Even if it meant coming in at three in the morning the rest of the week to catch up on their orders.

"Chase! Hey, man. Long time no see. How's it going?" Zach

asked from his spot where he was nailing stands into freshly cut trees.

"Busy," Chase said. "Looks like you can say the same."

Zach chuckled. "It's that time of year." He eyed Chase and, with a knowing look, said, "I heard you spent some time in Wonderland earlier this week. With Lily."

Chase stiffened. The last thing he wanted was rumors about them flying around Christmas Grove. "Who told you that?"

"Ilsa." Zach gave him a puzzled look. "Why? Was this information I wasn't supposed to know?"

"Oh, no. Nothing like that," Chase said. "It's fine. I just don't want the town gossiping about the fact that we spent the night together in Wonderland."

Zach raised an eyebrow. "Spent the night together?"

Son of a... Chase clamped his mouth shut and said nothing.

Laughing, Zach clapped him on the back. "It's fine, brother. I get it. I won't say another word other than I don't think the rest of the town knows anything. Ilsa knew, of course, because she picked Evan up and took care of him, and she told me why he was spending the night on a weeknight. I doubt she said anything to anyone else, except maybe Holly since all three of them are friends."

"Thanks, man," Chase said. "I appreciate that."

"No problem. Now, what can I do for you?"

Chase blew out a breath and rolled his shoulders, trying to ease his tension. "Looks like it's time to do the Christmas tree thing. What do you have in the eight-foot range?"

"Over this way." Zach jerked his head toward the far side of the lot.

Chase followed him and tried to keep his teeth from

chattering. "Damn, the temperature sure has dropped, hasn't it?"

"Looks like snow is coming sooner rather than later," Zach agreed. "I'm glad I don't have to drive anywhere."

"That's definitely a perk of living on the same land as the farm," Chase agreed. He quickly picked out a tree, and after paying, he and Zach hauled it out to his SUV. As they were strapping it to the top, Lily and her son Evan appeared in the parking lot that was closest to Zach and Ilsa's house. She and Evan must've been visiting with Ilsa and Vin.

Zach waved at her. "Get home safely, okay? I think the roads might already be icing up."

"We will," she called back. Her gaze shifted to Chase, and her eyes lit up. She smiled at him and gave him a slight wave.

Chase smiled back and had to stop himself from striding across the lot just to talk to her. Damn, he was a goner. He'd seen her every day since they'd been back in town because they worked together. But he hadn't had time to have a conversation that wasn't about orders or low inventory.

"Huh. That's interesting," Zach said.

"What is?" Chase asked while still watching Lily.

"Looks like something *did* happen in Wonderland."

Chase turned abruptly, causing the tree to shift and almost slide off the top of the SUV. "Dammit."

Zach just laughed and helped him get the tree back in place. "I guess I can think of a worse pairing."

"Gee, thanks. That's a ringing endorsement," Chase said dryly, not bothering to try to conceal the fact that he was indeed dating Lily. Or at least he would be once they had another date. She was going to try for Saturday night, but with the storm rolling in, it was a real possibility that they'd all be snowed in.

"You're welcome." Zach got busy tying the tree down and a few minutes later, he tapped the top of the SUV. "Looks like you're all set. Monday night, Rex and I are planning to head to the pub around seven. If you're free, maybe you could join us?"

Zach and Rex had invited him out a few times before, but it had never worked out. This time he'd make a point to be there. "Definitely. Text me with the time and place."

"Sounds like a plan." He waved and started to walk toward the structure that housed his office, but paused and peered back at the parking lot.

Chase followed his gaze and frowned when he realized Lily's car hadn't moved yet. In fact, she hadn't even started the engine. If she had, he'd see the gray air coming from her tailpipe. "Something's not right."

"I'll check on her," Zach said, already moving in her direction.

Chase followed, unable to leave without knowing everything was okay. The wind picked up again and chilled him to the bone. "Damn," he muttered. "It never gets this cold here."

"It's brutal," Zach agreed. He stopped at Lily's window and after a moment, he ran a hand through his dark hair. He glanced at Chase. "Glad you're here. Can you give us a hand? I think it might be the battery."

"Sure. I'll move my SUV over here. Be right back." By the time Chase had his SUV parked next to Lily's Kia, Zach already had jumper cables in his hands. Chase popped his hood open and waited for Zach's signal. Once he was ready, he started his car and waited.

Lily's car had zero response. They tried a few more times but quickly came to the conclusion that it must be electrical if they couldn't even get a spark.

Chase jumped out of his car and jogged over to Lily, who was now standing next to Zach with her arms crossed over her body as she shivered. Her sweater was doing nothing to keep the wind at bay. He quickly took his heavy jacket off and wrapped it around her shoulders.

"You don't have to do that," she said, even as she shoved her arms into the sleeves.

Chase shook his head. "I know. I wanted to do it anyway." He was wearing a sweatshirt with a T-shirt underneath. It wasn't enough, but it was better than what she'd been wearing.

"Is there someone you can call to take you home?" Zach asked. "I'd do it myself, but I'm the only one working the farm tonight. I can do it after we close, but who knows what the road conditions will be by then. Plus, I'm sure you want to get home to unwind."

"No, not really," Lily said, staring at Chase. "My dad would come if I asked, but I'm worried about him driving in the dark. His eyesight has been declining the past few years. A cab would be better."

"Cabs don't come out here," Zach said, also staring at Chase.

Chase didn't hesitate. "I can take you both. I'll even bring you back here to deal with your car as soon as possible."

Lily glanced up at Zach. "Is it okay to leave it here or do I need to call a tow?" She winced as she asked about a tow, and Chase was certain she didn't have the funds for that.

"Of course, it's fine," Zach reassured her. "Go with Chase. Stay safe through the storm, and we'll figure out what's going on with your car when the weather clears."

She just nodded, looking blank as if she hadn't processed anything he'd just said.

"Lily?" Chase asked. "Are you all right?"

"Yeah," she said quickly. "I'm just..." She let out a hollow laugh and waved at the Kia. "Car repairs. I have no idea how I'm going to handle that and Christmas, but I guess that's a worry for tomorrow." She glanced at the car. "Let me get Evan, and we can get going."

Chase wanted to tell her not to worry about the car. That he'd help her figure it out, but it wasn't his place. And something told him she'd resent him trying to swoop in and play the hero. However, if he could fix her car without having to have it towed into a shop, he knew she'd let him do that much. But like she said, that was a worry for tomorrow. Nothing was going to get done tonight.

"Come on, Evan. Mr. Garland is going to give us a ride," Lily said.

"We can't just leave the car here," Evan said.

"We'll come back for it tomorrow," she reassured him.

The boy walked in front of his mother, and when Chase opened the back seat for him, Chase said, "You can call me Chase. No need for Mr. Garland."

"Thanks," he said shyly and climbed into the car.

Lily gave Chase a grateful smile. "Thank you so much for... everything."

"It's my pleasure," he said, opening her door.

She swept past him, smelling of apple pie. It made him want to devour her right there in Zach's parking lot. Before she could even get into his SUV, fat snowflakes started to fall.

Evan let out a cry of delight. It was the first snow of the season in Christmas Grove. He couldn't blame the boy for being excited about it.

Lily took a moment to take in the snowflakes and then with a shiver, she climbed into her seat.

Chase turned to Zach. "Let me have a crack at the car before you call a tow truck, okay?"

"I'll do whatever Lily asks me to do," he said with his arms crossed over his chest.

"Good. She's lucky to have you in her corner," Chase said and then added, "I'll call you in the morning."

Once Chase was seated back in his SUV, he turned the heat up as far as it would go and rubbed his hands together. "Balls, it's cold out there."

Evan snickered while Lily grimaced. Chase had never seen her really shy away from a swear word. But then again, he hadn't really ever spent time with her while Evan was around.

Sorry, he mouthed to her.

She nodded and mouthed back, *Thanks*.

The drive from the tree farm back to town was slow going. The roads had indeed started to ice over, and the snow was coming down heavily. Chase took his time, trying his best to keep them from sliding off the road.

"You're good at this," Lily said, watching as he navigated the dicey roads.

"I've had practice. When you've lived your entire life in snow country, you pick some things up."

"I'd say so," she said and leaned her head back against the headrest, closing her eyes.

"Tired?" he asked.

"She's always tired," Evan interjected. "It's because she has to work too many jobs."

"I do not," Lily insisted. "Though with the hours I've been putting in at Love Potions, I am a little worn out."

"It's been quite the week," Chase said, unable to keep the hint of a smile off his face.

"It certainly has. Two broken down cars within days of each other. It's probably some weird curse," she said.

Chase agreed as he turned down the road that would eventually lead to her cottage. But just as he did, the line of cars in front of him came to a complete stop. Lily groaned and glanced at the navigation on her phone only to discover that even the reroutes were taking hours.

The storm intensified, and the wind was blowing the snow sideways, causing a near whiteout.

"Shi—I mean shoot," Chase muttered and quickly pulled the car to the side of the road. "There's no driving through this. Better to wait it out."

"Here? In the car?" Lily asked, her eyes wide with shock.

"No. Not in the car. We can walk to my place from here. It's just a few blocks down the road," Chase said. "That is, if you're okay with that."

Lily glanced at her son in the back and then at Chase. He saw the decision snap into place on her face just as she said, "As long as you'll let us help you with your tree."

He let out a surprised chuckle. "Do you really think I'll say no to that?"

"I didn't think so, but you never know." The three of them climbed out of the car and in no time, Chase had the ropes cut that were holding the tree in place. He hauled it off the roof of the SUV and then let Lily hold the lighter top end of the tree.

"Perfect. This way," Chase said.

It didn't take long to break out into a sweat. Hauling trees was serious business.

And by the time they were on Chase's front porch, all Chase wanted to do was cuddle up in the two-person swing that was hanging from a beam. Instead, he led them into the house and then checked the weather report.

His phone displayed a flashing red alert.

All roads closed until further notice. Residents of Christmas Grove need to shelter in place. Do not use the roads unless you absolutely have to. Storm won't pass until Sunday in the early morning hours.

Chase glanced up at Lily to find her reading the same weather alert. He gave her a tentative smile. "I have a spare room for both you *and* Evan."

"That's very kind, but—"

"Lily," he said softly. "Honestly, I don't think you have much choice. The roads are already closed."

She moved to look out the window and then glanced back at him. "It's already piling up."

Chase nodded and then wondered how he was going to get through the next night or two. With Lily under the same roof, how in the world was he going to keep his hands off her?

CHAPTER EIGHT

"*I*'m hungry," Evan said and plopped down into Chase's oversized chair next to the fireplace.

Lily frowned at the petulance she saw in his expression. He wasn't happy they were at Chase's house. It didn't really have anything to do with Chase, per se. It was because he wanted to be in his own room with his video games. And Chase had already broken the news that he wasn't a gamer.

"I'll rummage something up for dinner as soon as I get this fire going, buddy," Chase said cheerfully as he grabbed the basket on the hearth. "Give me about a half hour or so."

Evan cut his gaze to his mother. "Don't you have any snacks?"

Lily sighed. She knew if she didn't get something in her child, he was going to have a meltdown. While Evan was normally a sweet boy, when he needed fuel, he went from gentle puppy to growling, rabid wolf in two seconds flat. "No. I was just picking you up from Ilsa's and then we were going home." She turned to Chase. "Do you mind if I scavenge in your cabinets for a snack?"

Chase gave her an understanding smile. "Sure, go ahead."

"Thanks." Lily truly wanted to hug that man. He had no idea what he'd signed up for, having her and Evan for the next two days. She just hoped they didn't scare him off before they even got a start on their budding relationship.

Lily moved past the stairwell and took a left into the most beautiful kitchen she'd ever seen. The cabinets were a sea green color and accented with black granite counters and a gorgeous copper farmhouse sink. It was outfitted with a Sub-Zero refrigerator, a Wolf gas stove, and double ovens. She stood there, taking it all in, feeling a little like Alice in Wonderland. How had she ended up here in this gorgeous house with a gorgeous man who made her feel special in a way that no one ever had before.

"Mom!" Evan called. "I'm still hungry."

Lily rolled her eyes. It hadn't been that long since Ilsa had fed him. She genuinely wondered how her kid could burn so many calories in a day. If she ate like him, she'd be a walking beachball. "Come in here. I'll have a snack for you in a moment."

Her kid stomped into the kitchen, looking petulant. "Why do we have to stay here?"

"Because we're snowed in and Chase was kind enough to offer us his guest rooms," she said mildly.

"I'd rather have stayed with Vin." His arms were folded across his chest, and his chin was raised.

"I know, but we weren't expecting the storm to move in so fast." Lily found a jar of peanut butter and an apple. After slicing the apple, she put the pieces and a scoop of peanut butter on a plate. "Here. Sit at the table while you snack."

He grabbed the plate and started to walk back toward the living room.

"Evan. I said sit at the table," she said.

"I was going to ask Chase if he wants some," he said, acting innocent.

Lily shook her head. "He's busy. Just sit at the table. Chase will be in soon. If he wants some, I'll cut him an apple, too."

"Can I have a coffee?" Evan asked after he was sitting at the breakfast nook.

Good gods, what was she going to do with him? "Not tonight, Evan. I'll get you some water."

He let out a loud, heavy sigh and rolled his eyes at her, but he didn't argue and that was good enough for Lily.

"There's juice if you prefer that," Chase said, joining them in the kitchen.

Lily shook her head slightly, hoping Evan hadn't heard, but it was too late.

"Yes, I want juice," Evan said.

Lily grimaced and muttered, "Now you've done it."

Chase gave her a confused look and walked over to his fridge. "Done what?"

"You'll see," she said, shaking her head. She'd been trying to avoid the sugar rush that she knew would overtake her kid. He'd go from surly to bouncing off the walls if he had sugar before dinner.

"I've got cran-grape," Chase said.

Evan shrugged.

"Is that a yes?" Chase asked Lily.

She chuckled. "Yes."

He nodded and poured a glass for Evan. Lily watched as Chase brought Evan the juice and then sat down next to him.

Lily washed the knife and listened in while Chase tried to engage her son.

"I hear you're a pretty good baker," Chase said.

Evan shrugged again.

"If you want, later we can scour my cupboards for ingredients and see what we can make for dessert," Chase tried.

"I already had cookies at Vin's."

Lily couldn't help her chuckle.

Both Chase and Evan looked over at her.

She smiled at them both and asked, "How's it going?"

"Good," Chase said while Evan said, "Boring."

Lily nodded. "Sounds about right."

Chase shook his head and rose from the table. "How about I get dinner started?"

"Probably a good idea." Lily wiped her hands on a towel. "What can I do to help?"

Chase scanned the contents of his refrigerator. After a few moments, he said, "Pasta and meatballs, chicken quesadillas, or leftover stew?"

"Pasta," both Lily and Evan said at the same time.

"Pasta it is," Chase said, sounding relieved as he started to pull the ingredients and place them on the counter. Lily took a step back, waiting for instructions from the chef, while Evan came over to the sink and started washing his hands.

"Good job, buddy," Lily said softly.

He ignored his mother and went to stand next to Chase. "Can I make the meatballs?"

Chase blinked at him, obviously surprised, but Lily wasn't. He always helped her in the kitchen. When Chase glanced at her for confirmation, she nodded. He turned his attention to Evan. "Sure thing. Let me get you a bowl."

Evan nodded and waited patiently for Chase to hand him all the ingredients.

"Do you know what to do with all this stuff?" Chase asked him.

"Sure. Put it all in the bowl, mix it up, and then form meatballs." Evan said it as if any idiot should know how to make them.

Lily bit her lower lip to try to keep from laughing. If there was one thing that interested her kid besides video games, it was cooking and baking. He was forever under her feet in the kitchen. "How about I start working on the lights on your tree while you two handle this?"

Chase gave her a panicked look. "Uh, you don't have to do that. We can hang the lights together after dinner."

"It's really no problem," Lily insisted, recalling she'd spotted the boxes of lights on his coffee table when they'd walked in. "I'll just be in the way here. Besides, the lights aren't the fun part of decorating. I'll just get them on the tree, then we can do the rest later."

"If you're sure," he said, sounding anything but confident in the plan.

"I'm sure." Lily turned to Evan. "Be sure to listen to Chase and do whatever he asks. Remember, he's the chef and you're the assistant."

Evan nodded. "I know, Mom."

Chase chuckled. "I'm not sure I've risen to chef status, but I'll take it."

Lily patted his arm and said, "Good luck." Then she left the kitchen, grinning to herself that her two favorite boys appeared to be getting along. She didn't want to admit it, but it felt really good for the three of them to be together. It also touched her that Chase was making an effort to include Evan in their evening. Even Evan's own father had never shown much of an interest in doing anything with him. She shook her head, hating that she was constantly comparing Chase to Sean. That was too much pressure for anyone.

"Do you like onions?" she heard Chase ask Evan.

"No," he replied.

"I didn't either at your age, but I grew into them."

"Yuck."

They continued to talk about food. Mostly it was Chase trying to find out what Evan liked to bake. And once Chase got him talking about his favorite cupcakes, that was it. Her little chatterbox was going on and on about cupcakes, cookies, and muffins. Then he started in on wanting to try scones. All the while, Lily kept quiet and continued to layer on the Christmas lights. When it was lit up like the tree in Rockefeller Center, she took a seat and admired her handiwork.

It didn't take long for her eyes to grow heavy, and she closed them for just a moment.

"Lily?" Chase said, shaking her shoulder lightly.

"Huh?" She blinked up at Chase and into his amused bright-green eyes.

"Did you have a nice nap?"

She pushed herself up and glanced around, realizing that she must have fallen asleep. "Oh, gosh. I'm sorry." She glanced around frantically, looking for her son. "Where's Evan?"

"In the kitchen. He's finishing setting the table." Chase held his hand out to her. "Ready for some food?"

Lily let him help her up and regretted letting go of his hand as she followed him. Although they were staying with him while the storm passed, she didn't want Evan to think they were anything other than friends. It was way too soon for that. Still, she loved how easily they seemed to get along and couldn't help the flicker of hope that lit her up inside. If she finally let her guard down, was this what was waiting for her?

A cozy homelife with a man who went out of his way to care for her and her son? Tears pricked the backs of her eyes when she spotted Evan beaming at her from his spot at the table.

"Look, Mom," Evan said, pointing to the meatballs. "I cooked them myself."

"They look wonderful, sweetheart." She leaned over and gave him a kiss on his cheek.

"Ugh!" he cried, pulling away and wiping his face as if she'd just slobbered on him like a big dog. "You're embarrassing."

"That's what I live for." She beamed at him.

Evan shook his head, but the smile on his face gave him away.

"He's a terrific kitchen assistant," Chase said. "We even have some cookie dough chilling in the fridge. After dinner, we're going to get the cookie cutters out and pop them in the oven. When we're done with the tree, we can work on decorating them if you're up for it."

"That sounds... wonderful." Lily's heart was full, and the moment was so special she wished she could hold onto it forever. "Now, let's eat. I'm starving."

Chase dished out the pasta and meatballs while Evan passed the garlic bread they'd made.

Lily was very deliberate in taking a bite of the meatballs first, and when she did, she hummed her approval. "Evan, these are delicious. Great job, bud."

Her son flushed with pleasure and then dug in.

CHAPTER NINE

$\mathcal{C}$hase couldn't remember a time when he'd been so content to be snowed in. He genuinely enjoyed hanging out with Evan. The fact that they both had an interest in cooking and baking went a long way to form their friendship. What was remarkable was that their connection was completely outside of Chase's relationship with Lily. Chase just really enjoyed hanging out with Evan.

"Look, Chase," Evan said, holding up a gingerbread man who'd lost his head. Evan had frosted it so that the gingerbread man was wearing boots and had a dagger strapped to his waist. "It's the headless horseman."

"Ahh, the three wisemen and the headless horseman. Always a Christmas classic." He winked at Evan and went back to adding ornaments to the Christmas tree cookie in front of him.

Evan snorted and ate the head that was sitting in front of him.

Lily, who was still fussing with the Christmas tree, glanced at the clock and then over at her son. "Ten more minutes, then it's time to get ready for bed."

"But mom, we still have all these cookies to decorate," he complained.

"We can do them in the morning," Chase said, wiping his hands on a towel. "It'll give us something to do after we build a snowpeople family out back."

Evan didn't look impressed. "I've already built a snowman this year."

"Evan—" Lily started with clear disapproval in her tone.

"It's okay," Chase said, cutting her off. "I've already built one, too." He sent Lily a knowing smile. "There's always other things to do. I have a train set we can put up or—"

"You do?" Evan asked excitedly. "Is it electric?"

"It is," Chase confirmed. "It's a collection I started with my dad many years ago. It would be fun to get it back out again." Chase hadn't thought about those trains in years. In fact, he hadn't had them out the entire time he'd been married. His wife wanted everything to be modern and clean, even Christmas. Maybe that's why he'd gotten out of the habit of decorating. He hadn't liked Heather's style and found it too impersonal.

"Yes! Let's do that. I always wanted trains, but my dad said I was too young and my mom…" He glanced at his mother and clamped his mouth shut.

Lily got a sad expression on her face and said in a soft voice, "They aren't in our budget at the moment."

Chase nodded. "They aren't a cheap hobby. Not if you buy new, anyway. But I'm happy to share mine with you, Evan. Tomorrow we'll see what we can find, okay?"

Evan beamed. "Okay." He put the cookie frosting down and

stood. Then he ran over to his mother and gave her a hug and a quick kiss. "Night, Mom."

"Goodnight, sweetheart." She kissed the top of his head and added, "Don't forget to brush your teeth. I'll be up in a minute."

Chase had already fished out a couple of brand-new toothbrushes and put them in his spare bathroom for them. He'd even given them both a couple of his old T-shirts to sleep in, plus a pair of sweats for Lily. She wasn't excited about wearing the same clothes for multiple days, but she could do laundry, so it wasn't the end of the world.

Evan turned around and looked at Chase. He hesitated for just a moment and then ran over to him and wrapped his arms around his new friend, giving him a hug. "Night, Chase."

Chase ruffled his hair and in a gruff voice said, "Goodnight, bud. I had a good time tonight."

"Me, too." Evan held on for a moment longer and then ran up the stairs.

Chase glanced over at Lily and felt his heart squeeze when he saw the unshed tears in her eyes. "Lily?" he asked tentatively. "Is everything all right?"

She nodded and walked over to him. "Everything is perfect. I just..." She shook her head and leaned back in her chair. "You're very good with kids."

He let out a chuckle. "I don't know about that. Maybe it's just Evan. He likes the same things I do, so it's easy to hang out with him."

"Give yourself credit where credit is due, Chase," she said, holding his gaze. "Sure, your interests are aligned, but you are a natural at keeping him engaged and entertained. Even my dad isn't great at that. He would've spent maybe twenty minutes talking and then turned the television on."

"Hey, the television was my backup plan," he said. "In fact, it still is. I figure if we run out of stuff to do tomorrow, we can watch my favorite Christmas movie."

"Which one would that be?" she asked. "*Charlie Brown? The Grinch? Home Alone?*"

Chase snorted. "Please. The only Christmas movie on my must watch list every year is *Die Hard*. Yippee-ki-yay, mo—"

Lily cleared her throat loudly and nodded her head toward the stairs where Evan had appeared. "Do you need something, Evan?"

Her son glanced between Chase and Lily and finally settled his gaze on Chase. "I was wondering if I could borrow a book from your bookcase."

Chase glanced over at his built-ins. "Sure. Feel free to read anything you like."

Evan ran over to the bookcase and after a moment, he picked the first book in the Harry Potter series. He clutched it to his chest and retreated back to the stairs. "Thanks."

"Anytime," Chase said.

Lily rose. "I'll be right back."

Chase watched as Lily and Evan climbed the stairs. After they disappeared, he collected the trays of cookies, frosting, and sprinkles they'd used to decorate the cookies and got to work putting everything away. He was just finishing up when Lily reappeared in the kitchen doorway.

"Harry Potter is Evan's favorite series," she said.

"Isn't it everyone's?" he asked.

"Probably." Lily moved to stand next to him. "Is there anything I can do to help?"

"Nope. It's all handled. Unless you want an after-dinner snack. Cookie and some coffee maybe?"

"I won't say no to that," she said, already moving toward the coffeemaker. "Do you have decaf?"

"It's in the fridge." He retrieved the dark roast and a bottle of Irish Cream. He held it up in offering.

"Yes, please," she said and grinned at him. "You're one fine host. You know that, right?"

"I'm just being neighborly."

"Neighborly, huh?" She abandoned the coffeemaker and moved to stand in front of him. After slipping her hands around his waist, she gazed up at him and then pressed a soft kiss to his lips.

Chase's hands gripped her hips and pulled her in closer. It had been a very long three days since he'd felt her pressed against him. She tasted of sugar cookies and smelled like cinnamon, two things he could never get enough of.

"You smell like Christmas," she said with a contented sigh.

"Oh yeah? What exactly does Christmas smell like?" he asked.

"Vanilla, sugar, and a hint of pine." Lily clasped her hands behind his neck and kissed him again, only this time there wasn't anything soft about it. She pressed him against the counter and kissed him hard, her tongue eagerly seeking his.

Chase didn't hesitate to return her urgency. He knew what it meant to run his hands over her bare skin, to feel her under him, to hear the noises she made when she was filled with want and ecstasy. Chase wished desperately to experience every part of her again.

Lily froze, her mouth still pressed to Chase's. And then she suddenly untangled herself from his embrace and spun around as if looking to see if anyone was watching. Not *anyone*. Evan.

But when Chase followed her gaze, he didn't see anything other than the glow of the Christmas tree lights in the other room.

Lily pressed her hand to her chest. "Was he there?"

"I didn't see him."

She let out a breath. "I swear I heard him or something behind me."

"I didn't, but why don't you go check on him," Chase said, wanting desperately to touch her again, but she was far too tense. And Chase was certain that was the last thing she wanted in the moment.

"Yeah." She nodded and then took off up the stairs.

Chase pressed his hands down on the counter and blew out a breath. He was surprised to realize it hurt that she didn't want her son to know that they were dating. He understood where she was coming from and respected her decision, but it still stung a little.

"False alarm," Lily said softly. "He's in bed reading."

Chase glanced up to see her standing in the doorway again.

She had an apologetic look on her face. "I'm sorry."

He frowned. "For what?"

"I don't know." Lily glanced away, looking nervous. "You just seem a little upset."

Chase was gutted. He absolutely hated that his mood had made her feel like she needed to apologize to him. "Lily," he said softly and moved to stand in front of her. After taking her hands in his, he said, "You didn't do anything wrong."

She was frowning as she searched his eyes. "Then what is it? Is this all too much? We've sort of taken over your house. Maybe tomorrow we should try harder to give you some space. I don't know, maybe we can—"

"Lily," he said, cutting her off. "It's not too much, and I definitely wouldn't say you've taken over my house. I *like* that you're both here. It's nice to have you and Evan here helping me get ready for Christmas."

"Okay." She squeezed his hands. "Then what was wrong?

When I got back downstairs, you looked so... I don't know. Frustrated maybe?"

"Frustrated?" he echoed and realized he was going to have to tell her something other than the full truth. It was way too early in their relationship to tell her that he officially wanted to be her boyfriend and that it bothered him they had to keep it from Evan. He understood her reasons. And respected them. He just hadn't expected to like her and her son quite this much so quickly. "Listen, can we go sit in the living room?"

"Sure."

He held onto one of her hands as he led her into the other room, forgetting all about the coffee and cookies he'd promised her. Once they were seated, he turned to look at her in the glow of the Christmas lights. "Maybe I was a little frustrated. But not because of you. You didn't do anything wrong."

"Okay," she said. "What made you frustrated?"

"My late wife, if you can believe it." He let out a humorless laugh. "You know, everything about tonight is always what I thought my marriage would be like. Making cookies and decorating while the snow builds up outside is something out of a Hallmark movie, right?"

She nodded. "Yes. It did feel a little like that."

"With Heather, she would've already hired someone to decorate for us and wouldn't have taken the time to make Christmas cookies with me when the bakery down the street had *perfectly good cookies*." The last bit was said in a high-pitched voice as if he were imitating her tone. "It just hit me pretty hard that this evening with you and Evan was more enjoyable than any in the last few years that I was married." While he left out the part about being gutted by having to hide their budding relationship, he certainly wasn't lying. The evening had been everything he'd ever wanted. The only thing that could have made it better was if it were possible to wake up in the morning with Lily in his arms.

"Oh." Lily gave him a soft smile. "I get it. I feel the same way. Sean would've spent the evening behind his computer or on his phone. He'd never have made Christmas cookies or helped me decorate our tree. It's hard when you realize your marriage wasn't what you wanted it to be. Especially when you finally admit it wasn't anything close to what you deserved."

Damn. She'd just gotten right to the heart of how he felt about his marriage and hadn't been able to admit it to himself. He shook his head as he stared at her. "You know what, Lily Paddington?"

"What?"

"You're something else. Beautiful and smart. Come here." He tugged on her hand gently until she was pressed against his side.

She slipped an arm around his waist while pressing her other hand to his chest.

"I really want to kiss you again." He glanced over at the stairwell. "Would that be okay with you?"

She didn't even follow his gaze before she said, "More than okay."

Chase draped one arm over her shoulders and covered her hand against his chest with his own as he leaned in and brushed his lips over hers. They sat there together, kissing for a long while before Chase finally pulled back. They were both breathless. He gave her a sheepish smile. "I think maybe we should stop before we get too carried away."

She leaned in and kissed him once more before letting out a reluctant sigh. "Adulting sucks."

He chuckled. "No argument from me."

They stayed glued to each other, neither making a move to get up. Finally, Chase laid back against the cushions and pulled her with him until she was lying on his chest. He ran his fingers over the soft skin up her arm and along her neck.

"That's really nice," she said.

He kissed the top of her head and said a silent thanks to the universe for bringing them together.

CHAPTER TEN

"*T*ell us everything!" Holly Holiday demanded as she waved at the mugs of hot cocoa waiting for them on her coffee table. The new mom glowed with happiness as she cradled her daughter in her arms. The three-month old baby was sound asleep and looked adorable in her little elf costume with her splash of red hair peeking out from beneath the elf hat. It was a shade lighter than Holly's, but there was no mistaking they were mother and daughter.

The costume reminded Lily of her stay in Wonderland with Chase, and she couldn't help but smile at the memory.

"Uh-oh. What was that smile about?" Ilsa asked curiously as she took a seat in Holly's living room. She pulled her long dark hair up into a messy bun and then grabbed a mug for herself. It was Monday afternoon after the weekend snowstorm. Ilsa and Lily had stopped by to visit Holly and her daughter, Cleo, before they headed to Ilsa's where Zach was keeping an eye on Mia, Vin, and Evan.

"What smile?" Lily asked, trying to stall. She wasn't sure she even knew what to say about her time with Chase.

"That one," Holly and Ilsa said at the same time. They glanced at each other and laughed.

Lily grabbed her hot cocoa and took a sip instead of diving into her weekend.

Holly narrowed her eyes at Lily, studying her. Then she pursed her lips and asked, "Lil, is everything okay? Did something happen while you were at Chase's?"

"Huh? Yeah, I'm fine. Everything's good." She blew out a breath and covered her face with one hand.

"Doesn't look like everything is fine," Ilsa said.

Lily groaned. "I think I messed up."

"With who?" Ilsa asked. "Chase?"

Lily nodded, still covering her eyes with her hand.

"It didn't look like you messed up anything with him at work today. In fact, he couldn't keep his eyes off you," she offered.

"Really?" Lily peeked out from behind her hand.

"At one point he dipped his pen in chocolate instead of the biscotti and didn't even notice until I pointed it out on the tray," Ilsa said. "If that wasn't bad enough, he managed to make chocolate caramels that smoked and smelled like tobacco instead of lavender."

"Tobacco? We don't even have that flavor, do we?" Lily asked.

"Nope. His magic went haywire. I'm telling you, Lily, the man has it bad for you,"

Ilsa insisted.

Lily felt her lips turn up into a goofy smile. "He's really a good guy."

"Ah-ha!" Ilsa exclaimed. "Something *did* happen."

"Not this weekend!" Lily insisted. "I was there with Evan. We decorated his tree, made cookies, built snowmen in his yard, and then we played dominos. It was all very family friendly."

"Sure it was." Ilsa studied her. "But something happened in Wonderland, didn't it?"

Lily's cheeks flushed, and suddenly she was a lot warmer than she had been a few moments before.

"That's all the confirmation we need." Ilsa turned to Holly. "It looks like our girl has finally ended her dry streak."

Holly nodded and then frowned as her brows drew together.

"What's wrong, Hols?" Ilsa asked.

Holly clamped her lips together and shook her head. "I'm not sure exactly. Just a vision that doesn't make a lot of sense."

Lily's eyebrows shot up. "What was it? Did it have to do with me? Or Chase?"

Holly nodded and then grimaced. "I hate to even say anything because this one just can't be true. I'm not sure what to make of it."

"Have your visions ever been wrong before?" Lily asked.

"No. Though I have misinterpreted them due to lack of context." She shook her head. "Ugh, sometimes I hate this gift. It sucks."

"I know the feeling," Lily muttered.

Ilsa glanced between the two of them. "Okay, both of you are going to need to explain yourselves. It's no fun trying to guess what's going on in your heads. Lily?" she prompted. "Want to explain what you meant? Do you have a strange gift?"

Lily groaned. She didn't like to talk about this. But these ladies were her friends. If there was anyone she could tell her deepest secrets to, it was them. "I sometimes dreamwalk people I'm close to."

"People you're close to?" Ilsa asked. "What does that mean,

exactly? Friends, parents, siblings?" Her blue eyes glinted knowingly as she added, "Or are we talking about lovers?"

Dammit, Lily wanted the floor to open up and swallow her whole. This wasn't something she was ever comfortable talking about. "Only that last one," she admitted. "It's the reason my husband and I broke up."

"Because you invaded his dreams?" Holly asked, her gaze fixated on Lily.

"No, because it's how I found out he was having an affair," Lily said.

"Through his dreams?" Ilsa asked, her eyes wide. "Uh-oh. I dream about a lot of different men. Hopefully Zach is never privy to what goes on in my brain when I'm not in control."

"It wasn't like that. Or at least, I think I already suspected, and when he was dreaming about her, I got the vibe that it wasn't just dreams. So I started looking, and that's when I found out it was true," Lily explained.

"That bastard," Holly said under her breath.

"Jackass bastard," Ilsa added. "Anyone who would cheat on Lily is a major piece of—" She glanced at Cleo and rephrased what she had been planning to say. "Let's just say he's a dumb, selfish, egomaniac." She met Lily's gaze. "You deserve so much better, babe."

"Thanks, I think so, too." She turned her attention to Holly. "About that vision. Is it of the future?"

Holly nodded. "They always are."

"Come on, Hols," Ilsa urged. "What did you see? We're not letting you off the hook until you share with the class."

Lily nodded her agreement. "I showed mine, it's time for you to show yours."

"Fine," Holly said, still holding her child in her arms. "I saw Chase kissing another woman. Long blond hair, expensive black and red Christian Louboutin heels. And she was wearing a bodysuit that showed off every curve. I swear she looked just like that picture he has of his wife in his living room."

"But Chase's wife passed away," Lily insisted.

"Yeah, we heard about Heather," Holly said. "That's why I don't understand the vision. Is he going to be meeting with her ghost? Holding a séance?"

"Maybe he's consulting a Ouija board," Ilsa offered.

Lily shook her head at them. She had a hard time believing the vision was real. How could she? Chase's wife had died, so unless he was a necromancer, the odds were fairly low. "I don't think Chase would even want to talk to her, so if she were alive, I can't imagine him kissing her. Even before her untimely death, they were growing apart."

"I guess there's a first time for everything. Maybe the vision is flawed," Holly said. "In this case, I really hope it is, because if he hurts you, Lily, he's going to have to answer to me and my umbrella when I trip him walking down the street for the rest of time."

Ilsa snorted. "I like that visual. Maybe he can fall into a muddy snowbank and have to live in wet clothes all day, too."

"Hey," Lily said, trying to stop them. "Can we stop plotting Chase's demise? I'd like to at least give him a chance before one of us gets kicked to the curb."

"Sorry!" Ilsa said. "I hope the vision is wrong and you two end up married by New Year's with a tiny puppy curled at your feet every night."

"Guh, that sounds lovely," Holly said. "My New Year's will likely be spent changing diapers." But as she looked down at Cleo, it was obvious she wouldn't want to be anywhere else.

Ilsa reached over and took Lily's hand. "Hey, honey. I know

you're worried about what comes next. If I can just offer some advice?"

"Sure," Lily said.

"Try to take each day as it comes. And when it comes to Evan, he likely already knows something is going on even if he hasn't verbalized it. Your kid is smart. He won't miss the signals you two are giving off."

"I just don't want him to get attached," Lily explained. "It's one thing if Chase and I break up, but it's entirely another if he suddenly disappears from Evan's life."

Holly and Ilsa shared a knowing glance before Ilsa turned her attention to Lily. "Break up? Does that mean you're officially dating?"

"Yes." She nodded. "But Evan doesn't know. I don't want him getting attached if things don't work out."

Ilsa raised one eyebrow. "I think you might be too late already." Then she jerked her head toward the window. "Take a look out there."

Curious, Lily joined her by Holly's front window. Ilsa pulled back the curtain and waved at the three snowmobiles parked in a circle in Holly's front yard. Lily glanced back at them. "I only see snowmobiles."

"Uh, hun, look at who is waiting to climb on." Ilsa nodded to a small group patiently waiting their turns.

Lily immediately spotted Chase with Evan by his side. Zach and Vin were also there. The third would be occupied by a woman she didn't recognize. The only thing she could think to ask was, "Who's watching Mia?"

"Rex, probably," Holly said. "He went over to talk business plans with Zach earlier."

Lily found herself having to swallow her jealousy. While Ilsa and Holly were her friends, she'd never had the close-knit relationships that they had. She didn't have people to go play on the snowmobile with at all, much less last minute. And that hurt her soul. But as she gazed down at Chase and her son, who were climbing onto the snowmobile, she thought maybe she had the start of a circle. Chase was the start for both her and Evan.

"Who set up this excursion?" Lily asked them.

"Zach," Ilsa said. "He said they needed to run through the powder while it's still fresh, and the next thing I knew, they were getting them out of the garage. It's not a problem for Evan to ride one, is it?"

Lily shook her head. "No, not as long as an adult is looking out for him." Especially if that adult was Chase.

"Girl," Ilsa said. "You've got it bad."

"She really does," Holly said with a giggle.

It was then that Lily realized she hadn't taken her eyes off Chase the entire time she'd been at the window. She went to step away, but Chase suddenly glanced over her way and gave her that smile she loved so much. It was almost as if he felt her watching.

He gestured to Evan and mouthed, *Is this okay?*

Lily nodded and smiled back.

"Damn," Ilsa whispered from right beside her. "Whatever happened in Wonderland, I'm guessing the fireworks are still going off."

"Why do you say that?" Lily asked.

"Because, babe," Ilsa said, "the electricity sparking between you two is enough to power the entire town."

"Not everything is about chemistry," Lily said.

"No," Ilsa agreed. "But it sure doesn't suck." She winked at Lily. "Now come on. We have cookies to eat and more details to dish."

CHAPTER ELEVEN

*C*hase hadn't been intending to participate in a snowmobile ride. In fact, he'd only swung by the Christmas tree farm on a whim because Lily had mentioned they hadn't had a chance to get their own Christmas tree yet. He wasn't sure if it was time or a financial constraint, but either way, he wanted to surprise them with one as a thank you for helping him decorate his house. The train set he and Evan had put together had brought him more joy than he'd ever imagined. He just wanted to do something nice in return.

But when he'd walked into the Christmas tree farm after work, Zach was there with a friend and the boys, Vin and Evan. They were talking about snowmobiling, and when Evan spotted Chase, he'd begged him to join them.

How could he say no to that? He'd agreed immediately.

The tall, leggy, raven-haired beauty who was Zach's friend, walked over to him and held her hand out. "Hey, there. I'm Olivia, the woman who was the first to break Zach's heart."

"Uh, congratulations?" Chase asked, wrapping his large hand around hers.

She chuckled. "We were eight. But I'm pretty sure he's finally gotten over it."

Chase laughed. "I hope so. I'm Chase Garland. Nice to meet you."

Olivia swept her gaze over him, not doing anything to hide her interest. "You're not hard on the eyes, are you?"

"Uh, I don't—"

She threw her head back and laughed. "You're adorable. Tell me, Chase Garland, how and when did you end up in Christmas Grove, and why haven't I met you before now?"

"Oh, well, I moved here a little over a year ago to work as a chocolatier at Love Potions," Chase said, ignoring her flirty praise.

"Love Potions. Nice." She nodded in approval. "I bet you've got all kinds of tricks up your sleeve for wooing the ladies."

"Olivia," Zach said, shaking his head as he walked over to them. "Give the man a break. He's already spoken for."

"He is? Damn." It was her turn to shake her head regretfully. "And I was so looking forward to breaking his heart in a couple of months when I was done with him." She clasped Chase on the shoulder. "I hope you're not too disappointed."

"Only that I won't be in Zach's lonely hearts' club," Chase said, laughing along with them.

"I like him," Olivia said.

Zach turned to Chase. "Don't mind her. She's just feisty because she hasn't had anyone to harass for the last decade."

"That's because I was banished to the Midwest," Olivia explained. "But I ditched the deadweight and am back where I belong here in Christmas Grove where I can bust Zach's balls anytime I want to."

Chase stared at them and then narrowed his eyes. "If I didn't know better, I'd say you two were siblings, but since Olivia broke your heart when you were eight, I'm guessing there's no relation. Or have I stepped into some sort of *Twilight Zone* episode?"

"Our parents were best friends," Zach said. "We sort of grew up together before Olivia ran off to college and then got married to the farmer." He eyed her for a moment and then teased, "I guess it's good to have you back."

Olivia made a show of pretending to sock him in the arm. "You know you missed me."

Zach draped an arm over her shoulder and pulled her in for a sideways hug. "Sure. Now we have another babysitter option when Ilsa and I need a night out."

She chuckled. "You're presumptuous, but I suppose a night in with Mia and Vin wouldn't be terrible."

"I knew you'd see it my way," Zach said.

The entire time Chase watched them he felt a pang of envy. He'd had friends of course, but hadn't ever had that sort of connection before. What would it be like to know someone that well?

"Dad!" Vin called as he ran to one of the snowmobiles. "Can we go now?"

Zach squeezed Olivia's hand. "Time to roll." Then he glanced over at Vin and called back, "Sure, buddy. Let's ride."

"You two are toast, Frost!" Olivia called after Zach. "Hope you like the taste of snow."

Laughing, Zach jogged over to Vin and helped him put his helmet on.

Chase glanced around for Evan and found him standing awkwardly next to the third snowmobile, just waiting. Chase walked over and placed a hand on his shoulder. "Are you ready to fly through the snow?"

Evan bit down on his lower lip and stammered when he asked, "D-do we have to go fast?"

"No, not if you don't want to," Chase said, realizing that Evan probably hadn't ever been on one of the snowmobiles before. "We can go at our own pace."

"Even if they're racing?" He gestured to Olivia, Zach, and Vin.

"Absolutely. We can do whatever we want." Chase handed him the smaller helmet that was on the seat. "All you need to do is put this helmet on, and then we can test this baby out."

"Just don't go too fast, okay?" he asked, his blue eyes wide with worry.

"We'll go at whatever speed you're comfortable with." Chase put on his own helmet, checked to be sure Evan's was on properly, and then climbed onto the machine. He nodded to Evan. "Take the seat behind me and hold on tight."

Evan climbed on behind him, and when he wrapped his arms around Chase, he wondered of the kid was going to bruise a rib. But instead of forcing him to loosen his grip, he just patted Evan's hands and asked, "Ready?"

"Ready," Evan said, his voice muffled.

Chase eased into the throttle, taking it slow like Evan requested. The moment the machine started to move, Evan tightened his death grip, making Chase let out a small grunt of pain. How was the kid was so strong that he felt like he was going to lose a rib?

Zach and Vin whizzed by with Vin yelling and waving to Evan. To Chase's surprise, Evan didn't even release his death grip to wave at his friend. A moment later, Olivia shot by them. She was leaning forward as if willing the snowmobile to go faster.

Chase took it easy as he promised, and it wasn't long before

Evan loosened his hold and was chatting animatedly about the trees, the snow, and the various wildlife that could normally be seen in the woods. Chase enjoyed every moment of it, and when the sun started to hang low in the sky, he reluctantly turned back toward Holly's house and the Christmas tree farm.

"Stop, stop, stop!" Evan ordered.

Thinking there was something wrong, Chase slowed to a stop and then spun around. "What is it?"

"Shh." Evan held his finger to his lips and nodded toward a clump of trees off to the right.

Chase followed his gaze and then relaxed when he noticed a herd of reindeer standing still, watching them. It was rare to see reindeer in Christmas Grove, but not unheard of. He pulled out his iPhone and quickly took a dozen or more photos to commemorate the experience.

They stayed still, just watching and waiting, until the herd raised their heads as if they heard something. Suddenly they broke out into a run, each one sprinting deeper into the woods.

"It's too bad Mom wasn't here," Evan said. "She'd have loved to see them."

"I bet she would've," Chase agreed. "Maybe we can do this again when she has some time."

"Can we?" Evan asked, his voice raised in excitement.

Chase grimaced to himself, knowing he shouldn't be making plans for anything with Evan without speaking to her first. "We'll have to ask her, bud."

"Oh." His shoulders slumped. "She won't ever be able to."

"Why?" he asked, concerned about Evan's change in mood. "I thought she liked the outdoors?"

"She's always working," he said flatly.

"Not in the afternoons though, right?" Chase asked.

91

"She's usually at the train store in the afternoon," Evan said, his voice full of resignation. "Or at the tree farm."

"Really?" Chase knew she sometimes worked at the tree farm, but he'd thought that was more just to help out Zach and Ilsa.

"She says she needs to. Can we go now? I'm hungry."

"Sure, Evan." Chase powered up the snowmobile and was just getting ready to head back to the clearing when he saw something move off to his left. He focused on the clump of trees, expecting to see more reindeer. Only he didn't see any wildlife at all. Instead, he spotted a man with a camera, retreating back into the woods on foot. It looked like they weren't the only ones who'd stopped to enjoy the reindeer.

The ride back to the clearing didn't take long, and just as they were climbing off and ditching their helmets, Zach, Vin, and Olivia came racing in. They were yelling at each other good naturedly, each insisting they were going to win the great snowmobile reunion race. But before they came to a stop, Olivia seemed to slow down to let Zach and Vin win. Vin jumped off the snowmobile and started running around with his hands in the air, jubilant in their victory.

Olivia grinned at him while Zach gave Vin a high five.

"She let them win," Evan said with a fair amount of judgment in his tone.

"It seems she did. Wasn't that wonderful of her?" Chase asked him.

"Why? It's not really winning if she threw the race."

"That's one way of looking at it," Chase said. "And certainly, if this was an official event like the Olympics or a national competition where careers or prize money was on the line, then it would be a bigger deal. But Olivia's kindness just made a young boy's day. It cost her nothing to let him win. And in return, she gets to share in his joy. What's more important? Winning or bringing joy to other people in big and small ways?"

"I never thought of it like that before," Evan said. "That's actually really cool."

"I think so, too," Chase said and clapped him on the back, his heart swelling at the connection he was making with Lily's kid. He'd always wanted a family, but he hadn't really understood just how fulfilled he could be by being present in a child's life.

"Hey," Lily said, strolling off Holly's porch toward them. "Looks like you two had a good time."

"It was fantastic, Mom!" Evan exclaimed as he ran over to her. "You should've seen the herd of reindeer. They were just standing there like they were waiting for us. Chase took a bunch of photos, but we should really go out again so you can see them too."

Lily's eyes glittered with amusement at her son's animated enthusiasm. "That sounds fun, but it's too late today. The sun's already setting, and we need to get home and get some dinner."

"Can Chase come?" Evan asked. "He got us a tree."

She frowned and then stared at Chase as she asked, "He did what?"

"He got us a Christmas tree. So he's stopping by to drop it off. We have to invite him to dinner. It's the polite thing to do, right?" Evan insisted.

Her lips pressed into a thin line, indicating she was irritated. But still, she said, "Yes. That is the polite thing to do. Chase, would you like to join us for dinner? It's tomato soup and grilled cheese night."

Chase wasn't exactly sure what had irritated her. Was it the tree or that she now felt forced to invite him over? Either way, he didn't want to force himself on her. "I don't want to impose."

"You're not!" Evan called as he walked over to where Vin and Zach were still talking to Olivia.

Once he was out of earshot, Lily turned on Chase. "We don't need you to buy us a tree. I'm going to get one when I get paid next."

He blinked at the sudden harshness in her tone. Then he did a mental calculation on when they'd be getting their next checks from Love Potions. "That's right before Christmas."

"So? A lot of people trim their trees on Christmas Eve," she insisted. "I don't need you to take care of us, Chase. I've got it handled."

"Right." He held his hands up in surrender, suddenly understanding why she was so irritated with him. She obviously didn't want to be seen as a charity case. And while he knew that they struggled to make ends meet, that hadn't been his intent at all. "I'm sorry. I didn't mean to impose. I just wanted to thank you for all your help making my house festive for the holiday this weekend. I wasn't trying to do anything other than say thank you."

"Oh." She let out a breath as the fight seemed to drain out of her. "That's a kind gesture but completely unnecessary."

"I understand. I guess I can put a second one in my house. There's room in the kitchen. Though I don't have any more decorations. Honestly, Lily, it's going to cost me more to keep it because I'm going to have to hit the Christmas store for more ornaments. At this point, you'd be doing me the favor by taking it off my hands."

She shook her head in mock exasperation. "You're a smooth talker. Ordinarily, that kind of talk wouldn't work on me, but since you've already told Evan, he'll be disappointed if he has to keep waiting. Go ahead and bring the tree over. And stay for dinner if you want."

"Why, thank you," he said, miming a tip of his hat. "I'll definitely take you up on that offer."

They were silent as they crossed the clearing to retrieve Evan.

Just before they reached her son, Lily stopped and turned to him. "I think I need to apologize for getting upset about the tree."

"You don't," Chase said, giving her an understanding smile.

"Yeah. I think I do. Since when have I become so ungrateful? Thank you for thinking of us and getting us a tree. Evan will love it." She brushed her long blond hair out of her eyes. "And so will I."

"You're welcome." Chase wanted to pull her into his arms and let her know that there was nothing he wouldn't do for her, but he knew it wasn't the right time. Not there in front of everyone, and not when she was clearly uncomfortable with anyone trying to take care of her and her son. He admired her independence, but he still wanted to ease her burden. He just hoped that one day she'd let him.

CHAPTER TWELVE

*L*ily was so conflicted about having Chase at her house. On the one hand, she was thrilled to be spending more time with him. He was kind and seemed to genuinely enjoy spending time with Evan. The problem was that all of the lines she'd drawn were now blurred. Even though Evan had no idea she was dating Chase, the pair of them were getting closer and closer. And that scared her.

What if things didn't work out? What if Chase decided it was too much to be dating a woman with a child? Or if Chase didn't feel the same way about her as she did him? It was great that he liked her son, but if they didn't work out, what would that do to Evan? He'd already been abandoned by one man who was supposed to love him. Lily couldn't take it if it happened again.

"Where do you want this?" Chase asked. He was standing in her doorway, holding the tree he'd gotten for her.

"Over here!" Evan ran across the living room and pointed

at the space between the fireplace and the sliding glass door. "That way we can see the lights when we're outside."

Chase glanced at Lily for confirmation. She nodded and hung back while they got it set up in the Christmas tree stand.

"What do you think?" Chase asked her. "Is it straight?"

Lily eyed it, gave instructions for it to be moved toward the right, and then flashed a thumbs-up when it was about as straight as it was going to get. The noble fir was gorgeous and filled the space perfectly. Tears stung the backs of her eyes. She felt foolish getting choked up over a tree, but the truth was she knew there was no way she'd have been able to afford one that lovely. Add in the fact that Chase had cared enough to go out of his way to bring them a tree because he knew they didn't have one, and she was ready to ugly cry right there in her living room.

"Mom, where are the decorations?" Evan demanded.

"In the garage. I'll go get them," she said.

"We've got it." Evan grabbed Chase by the hand and started tugging him in the direction of their one-car garage.

Chase glanced back at Lily.

"In the tote on the workbench," she said.

He nodded. "We'll be right back."

Lily watched them go and then went into her small kitchen to start dinner. The house she rented was a small two-bedroom cottage that was built in the fifties. The white kitchen cabinets were original and had a certain amount of charm. But there wasn't anything fancy about the Formica counters and linoleum floors. While it was clean and tidy, it was a far cry from Chase's fancy custom cabinets and granite counters. She sighed, feeling inadequate. It always seemed that no matter how hard she tried, she never seemed to get ahead. There were always school clothes to buy or doctor's appointments to cover. And with no help from Sean, fancy kitchens were a pipe dream.

"After we do the tree, can we build another snowman?" Evan asked Chase as they hauled the Christmas tote into the living room.

"It's a school night," Lily called as she walked from the kitchen to the living room. She leaned against the wall with her arms crossed over her chest as she added, "After dinner, we can finish the tree, but then it'll be time to get ready for bed."

"But, Mom," Evan whined, "Chase is here."

"You spent this afternoon with Chase," she said. "We can build a snowman this weekend."

Evan turned to Chase with big puppy dog eyes. "Can you come this weekend?"

"We'll see, kiddo," Chase said.

"Aww, Chaaaase," Evan said.

Lily cleared her throat. "Evan, that's enough. Don't pressure Chase. I'm sure he has other things to do this weekend besides spend it with us."

Her son narrowed his eyes and stared at Chase. "Like what?"

Lily also wanted to know what might be occupying his time. Did he really have plans, or was he just getting tired of entertaining Evan? She wondered if he might even be getting tired of her. He had been spending a lot of time with them lately. She couldn't blame him for wanting a little space.

Chase chuckled. "Grown-up things, buddy."

Evan let out a disappointed sigh but then rallied. He turned to his mom. "Can we play video games until dinner's ready?"

Lily shook her head in amusement. Her kid was normally shy, but there was nothing shy about him when he was with Chase. "You'll have to ask Chase, but dinner will be ready in about ten minutes, so whatever you do, make it quick." She gave Chase a sympathetic look and said, "Good luck."

"Sounds like I'm gonna need it," he said good-naturedly.

Chuckling, Lily disappeared back into the kitchen and started cooking their grilled cheese sandwiches. It wasn't long before she heard the unmistakable sound of Evan's favorite video game playing in the living room.

Once she had the grilled cheese and tomato soup on the table, she called out, "Time's up. Dinner's ready."

"Coming!" Evan called and a moment later ran into the kitchen.

"Hands," Lily said.

Evan immediately retreated to the hall bathroom where he washed his hands. Once he was done, he told Chase, "Your turn."

Chase nodded and went to wash his hands. When he returned, Lily and Evan were already seated at the table, waiting for him.

Lily grinned at him. "Welcome to the Paddington household. Aren't you glad you decided to visit?"

"You have no idea how much," he said seriously. "However, I am rethinking the video games. I don't think I've ever been that bad at anything before."

Evan snickered. "He's really terrible."

"You're in good company," Lily reassured Chase. "When you look up video game disasters on the internet, I'm listed first."

Evan rolled his eyes.

Chase laughed. "Well, now they can add me. We make a good pair."

It was ridiculous how much Lily loved that he'd said they were a pair. It also surprised her how much she loved just having him in her house. For years after she left Sean, she wondered if she'd ever be able to share her space with someone other than Evan. The very idea hadn't been appealing at all. However, Chase just felt... right. She glanced away from him, worried that everything she was feeling in that moment was written all over her face.

"You're not eating it right," Evan informed Chase.

Chase looked down at his soup and frowned. "Is there some other way than with a spoon?"

"You have to dip your sandwich in the soup," Evan said as if that was obvious. The two bantered back and forth about the best way to eat their dinner, while Lily sat back and watched them.

When they were done, the three of them decorated the tree. It didn't take long, since Lily's collection of ornaments was relatively small. Evan lost interest after placing two ornaments on the tree and then curled up on the couch with his nose in a Percy Jackson book.

Once they finished, Lily stood back and wrinkled her nose. "It definitely could use some more ornaments to fill in these spaces."

"I think it looks nice," Chase said. "It's sort of minimalist. Nothing wrong with that."

"It needs candy canes," Evan said.

"That can probably be arranged," Chase agreed.

Lily glanced at the clock. "Ev, it's time to get ready for bed."

"Just one more chapter," he said.

"You can read it in bed after you brush your teeth," she said, knowing that if she gave in, he'd just keep pushing.

"Fine." Clutching the book, he disappeared into the bathroom.

Lily smiled ruefully at Chase. "This isn't exactly the kind of dating I had in mind."

"Is that what this is? A date?" he asked, raising one eyebrow.

How was she supposed to answer that? "I don't really know."

He moved to stand right next to her and squeezed one of her hands. "I think this is what it looks like when someone is dating a woman with a kid."

Lily swallowed. "This isn't how I thought this was going to go."

"I know. Does it bother you that I've spent so much time with Evan?"

She shook her head. "No. I thought it would, but it doesn't. It's really nice watching the friendship between you two."

"I'm really glad to hear that. He's a special kid."

Lily's heart melted right then and there. She was tired of telling herself that she had to keep her distance from him. That she needed to protect her son. Deep down, she thought maybe she was also protecting herself. "He is a special kid who deserves the best."

"He already has the best with you, Lily. You're a great mom."

That was it. She was done for. Lily gazed up at him and wondered how it was possible that this man had come into her life.

Evan came running back into the living room and barreled into Lily, giving her a hug. "Goodnight, Mom."

"Night, baby."

He let go of her and spun into Chase, giving him a big hug, too. "Goodnight," he muttered.

"Goodnight, Evan."

Evan released him and then ran back down the hall to his bedroom.

"I'll be right back," Lily said and followed her son. After she tucked him in and kissed him goodnight, she closed the door behind her as she retreated back to the living room.

Chase was sitting on the couch in the dark with just the glow of the Christmas tree lights illuminating him. Lily took a seat next to him. Her nerves were all over the place, and it made her feel ridiculous. She knew this man intimately. Their night in Wonderland had been magical. Why was she so nervous now?

Wonderland had been a stolen moment in time, but now she was in her house, with her kid, and it didn't get any more real than it was in that moment.

Chase draped an arm over her shoulders and leaned in closer. "Are you okay?"

She blew out a breath. "Yeah. Reality is just sinking in."

"What do you mean by that?" he asked.

She waved a hand toward the hallway. "Just the realities of dating while being a mom. I don't really know what I'm doing."

"You don't have to. We'll figure it out together." Chase cupped her cheek and moved in, giving her a soft kiss. Lily let out a contented sigh and then kissed him back, getting completely lost in him... right up until her phone rang, startling them both.

Lily jerked back and fished her phone out of her pocket. When she saw the number on the screen, her entire body went ice-cold.

"What's wrong? Who is it?" Chase asked.

"My ex." Lily jumped up and strode into the kitchen as she answered. "Sean?"

"Hello, Lily," he said.

"What do you want?" she asked, her tone full of acid.

"Well, happy holidays to you, too," he said with a chuckle. "Can't the father of your child call to talk about gifts for his son?" His tone made her stomach churn. He'd turned the charm on the way he used to when he was getting ready to railroad someone.

"You can call anytime, but you never do, so forgive me for being a little cold. Your son deserves better," she said.

"Seriously?" All the charm was gone now. "You have some nerve to tell me my son deserves better from *me*. What about *you*?"

"Me? What in the sweet hell are you talking about? Everything I do is for Evan. Where have you been the last three years?" Lily was fuming mad. Was he really calling to criticize her parenting after he'd been MIA for so long?

"So bringing your boy toy around is for Evan?" he spat out. "How dare you leave my child in the care of some stranger?"

Lily was so angry she was shaking. "What in the hell are you talking about?"

"I'm talking about the man who's currently in your house. The one who took him snowmobiling today while you were nowhere to be found. That's what I'm talking about."

A cold chill ran down Lily's spine. She clutched the phone so hard her hand started to cramp. "How do you know who is in my house right now?" she asked through clenched teeth.

"That's irrelevant. I'm just calling to let you know I'm picking my son up on Saturday and keeping him until New Year's Day."

"The hell you are. You haven't seen him in three years. You can't just come take him from me."

"We have shared custody, Lily. Remember that?" he said

coolly. "I can and I will. Have him ready to go by 10:00 a.m. And make sure your *boyfriend* isn't there."

"There's no way that's happening," Lily said, her voice shaking with anger.

Silence met her on the other end of the line.

"Sean?"

No answer.

The phone beeped twice, indicating that the call had ended.

Lily stared at her phone in shock and then threw it down on the counter as she spat out, "Son of a... ugh!"

CHAPTER THIRTEEN

"*L*ily?" Chase placed a hand on the small of her back. She was shaking so violently that he wanted to go into protector mode and do whatever it took to get her ex out of her life. But he knew that wasn't what she needed. She didn't need a savior; she just needed a friend and a confidant. "What did he want?"

She lifted her head. The anger and fierce determination on her face reassured him. Whatever had happened, she wasn't going to lay down and just take it. "He wants Evan, starting Saturday and through New Year's."

"He just sprung that on you out of the blue?" Chase asked.

She let out a humorless bark of laughter. "Yeah. He thinks he can just call and dictate to me what he wants. After no contact for almost three years. Who the hell does he think he is?"

"Evan really hasn't seen his dad at all in three years?" Chase asked. He knew she'd talked about Sean not being active in Evan's life, but he hadn't realized she was speaking literally about him being completely MIA.

"Nope. He hasn't paid child support either, the bastard."

"Whoa." Anger curled in Chase's gut. It was intense, and he had no idea what to do with it. He sucked in a deep breath. "Okay. Obviously, you're not going to just let this happen. What can I do to help?"

She shook her head. "I don't know. We have joint custody, so it's not like I can keep Evan from him, even if he has been an absent father. But how is it fair that he just gets to call and berate me about my choices and then try to tell me what to do?"

"Berate you? About what?"

Lily clenched her jaw before she said, "You. He somehow knew that you and Evan were snowmobiling today, and he was pissed that I'd let Evan spend time with *some stranger*." She raised her hands in air quotes. "How does he know that?"

Chase was completely taken aback, and it took him a moment to collect his thoughts. "He doesn't live around here, right? Didn't you tell me he moved Back East?"

She nodded.

"Does he have a friend around here keeping an eye on you and Evan or something?" Chase wondered.

"I really don't know. Maybe. We lived down in Sacramento when we were married, so it's not out of the question. But what I really don't understand is, why would he care? Why, after three years, is he suddenly worried about what we're up to?"

"I wish I knew the answer to that." Chase was really bothered by the news that her ex, who didn't even live in the state, somehow knew he and Evan had spent the day together. He didn't care if the man knew, he cared about how he found out. That was a very short amount of time for him to have been informed about something that was so innocuous.

"Oh, gods," Lily said. She bent over at the waist as if the entire situation was giving her a stomachache. "What am I going to do?"

This time Chase didn't hesitate. He wrapped her in his arms and whispered, "It'll be okay. We'll figure this out. I promise."

She turned into him and buried her face in his chest. Finally she forced out, "I don't think I have a choice. I can't keep Evan from him."

He ran his hand over her back. "I think you need to talk to a lawyer tomorrow."

She shook her head.

"Why?" Chase asked, pulling away so he could look her in the eyes.

Lily grimaced and glanced away. "I can't afford a lawyer."

Because the bastard had stopped paying her child support. "I'll help you find someone. There has to be some family lawyers who work pro bono around this area."

"I wouldn't even know where to start," she said, wiping at her eyes. "I didn't even have a lawyer when we got divorced. We used a mediator."

"We'll figure it out together," Chase said.

"You're being really sweet." Lily pressed her hand to his chest. "But I don't want to bother you with this. It's not your problem."

Chase swallowed his frustration and took her by the hand, leading her back into the living room. Lily sank down onto the couch and stared at the tree.

"I'll be right back." Chase retreated to the kitchen and scrounged around until he found some instant hot cocoa packets. A few minutes later, he carried two mugs back into the living room. "Here. Drink this."

Lily took it and held it in both hands.

Chase sat next to her. "I would've spiked it, but I couldn't find any booze."

"There isn't any," she said. "I don't drink often."

While Chase was sure that was true, he also noticed that her kitchen was stocked mostly with generic items and foods that were kid friendly. In fact, her entire house centered on Evan's wants and needs. There didn't appear to be anything extra for Lily. It was clear she rarely spent money on herself, and it only made him want to support her more.

He draped an arm around her and pulled her in until she rested her head on his shoulder.

They sat in silence for a while until Lily let out a quiet sigh. "I need to tell Evan his dad wants to see him."

"I'm sure he'll be happy about that."

She nodded. "I'm sure he will, but what about when Sean disappears again?"

"Do you think that's what he'll do?" Chase asked. "If he's so insistent about seeing him now, maybe he wants to rebuild a relationship with Evan."

Lily let out a skeptical grunt. "His history says otherwise."

"Fair enough."

"That's why I think if I just let him take Evan for a couple of weeks, he'll lose interest and that will be that," Lily said, sounding completely defeated.

Chase had a bad feeling in the pit of his stomach. He didn't know her ex at all, but what he did know was that he was a man who'd deserted his family and was now trying to bully her into letting him do whatever he wanted. It made Chase worry about what he might try next. Lily couldn't just take what he was doing lying down. She needed to be protected. "That might be true, but what happens if he starts dictating other things? What if he decides he wants to exercise his joint custody and demands that happens Back East?"

She jerked up and turned to face him. "He wouldn't."

"Are you sure?"

Lily covered her face with her hands and muttered, "I can't think about this right now."

"Okay," Chase said. "You don't have to." Because if she couldn't, he would do it for her. There was no way he was going to let her ex waltz into Christmas Grove and take over their lives. One way or another, he'd make sure she was protected.

There was an awkward silence until Lily stood and said, "I think maybe it's time to call it a night."

Chase rose and placed one hand on her hip and caressed her cheek with the other. "I know you've got a lot on your mind, but just know that I'm here for you."

She closed her eyes and leaned into his touch. "Thank you for that."

"I want to reassure you that everything will be okay, but I know those words feel empty right now. So instead, I'll just tell you that you're strong. Stronger than anyone I know. And I know that in the end, you'll do whatever is best for Evan. You always do."

Lily opened her eyes. Unshed tears shone in the light of the Christmas tree. "You have no idea how much I needed to hear that."

"It's just the truth," he reassured her.

"Thank you." Lily wrapped her arms around him and hugged him with everything she had. After a few moments, she leaned in and kissed him.

Chase held her close and let her take the lead. When she deepened the kiss, he went all-in with her, burying his hand in her hair and pulling her in until she was pressed against him. They kissed for a long time, hands clutching and roaming, but neither took it further.

Finally, when Lily pulled away, she leaned in and pressed her cheek against his chest and said, "Thank you for being here tonight."

"Always," Chase said, holding her close.

She glanced up at him. "Call me tomorrow?"

"Absolutely." Chase kissed her again and then pulled away, understanding that she was ready for him to leave. "Try to get some sleep."

"I will."

"If you have trouble, you can always call me. I'll pick up," he said.

She gave him a grateful smile. "I just might do that."

He squeezed her hand once, kissed her one more time, and reluctantly left. If it were up to him, he'd have stayed and held her all night. But he respected that Lily needed her space and needed to come to terms with what she wanted to do about her ex.

Although that didn't stop him from firing off an email when he got home. He just cared too much about Lily and Evan to stand by and let her ex hurt either of them.

CHAPTER FOURTEEN

*L*ily didn't sleep at all. She'd put herself to bed and then tossed and turned all night as her thoughts raced. She was still in shock that Sean had called and demanded time with Evan. That had been the last thing she'd expected. Her biggest and most important question was whether Sean really wanted to see Evan or if he was just doing this to hurt Lily.

Sean would know just how hurtful it would be to demand Evan over Christmas. A small voice in the back of her head told her he was only doing this because he'd somehow found out she was seeing Chase. That was something he clearly had a problem with, considering the phone call they'd had the night before. If that was the case, what else would Sean do to punish her for moving on with her life?

She crawled out of bed and pressed a hand to her stomach. She'd had an ache in her gut since the night before that just wouldn't go away. Lily suspected it wasn't going anywhere anytime soon. Not until she found out exactly why Sean was in town and why it was suddenly so urgent for him to see Evan.

The phone rang, and Lily tensed until she saw her dad's number flash on the screen. "Hey, Dad. What's up?"

"Morning, Lil. I'm calling because band practice was canceled, and I have the afternoon free. I was hoping Evan is free for a little Christmas shopping."

"Sure," she said. "Are you picking him up from school? If so, I'll let Ilsa know she doesn't need to wait for him."

"Yep. I'll be there with bells on."

"I think you can leave the bells at home. What happened with band practice?" Her dad was a part of a classic rock band called the Colossal Fossils. They were the go-to band for Christmas Grove weddings and parties. They were pretty decent for a cover band. Not quite as good as the band in *The Wedding Singer*, but they did all right.

"Percy says he has laryngitis, but we're pretty sure he just wants to take Bambi Boots to Boomtown for a gambling tournament."

"Who could resist anyone named Bambi Boots?" Lily asked with a chuckle.

"Not Percy. Last month she talked him into going to a B&B called The Cat's Meow. She posted pictures of him covered in five cats while sitting on a pink velvet couch."

Lily couldn't hold in a laugh. "I have trouble imagining that."

"Oh, no," her dad assured her. "It's one hundred percent true. Harry printed copies out, and we're going to sell prints at our gigs."

"You guys are ridiculous."

"Maybe, but we have fun. Okay, gotta run. I'll have Evan home in time for dinner."

"Sounds great. Love you."

"Love you, too."

The line went dead, and Lily looked up to find Evan staring at her.

"Hey, buddy. Your grandpa is going to pick you up from school today. How do you feel about that?" she asked, giving him a warm smile.

Evan stared at her with narrowed eyes.

"What?" She poured him a glass of orange juice while she waited.

"Are we going somewhere for Christmas?" he asked with his arms crossed over his chest.

"No, why?" she asked, hating that she'd sort of just lied to him. She wasn't going anywhere, but he likely would be. If Sean was insistent on seeing him for Christmas, she suspected that even if she did lawyer up, she'd lose that battle after having him all to herself for three years.

"Then why can't I go on the overnight trip to Lake Tahoe with my class?"

Oh, hell. Lily pressed a hand to her forehead, silently cursing herself. When she couldn't sleep the night before, she'd caught up on email. One was from Evan's teacher with a permission slip to join the class for an overnight trip that included a winter hike through the woods. The cost was minimal since one of the parents ran a summer camp and had enough cabins to accommodate the entire class. So money wasn't the issue. But she'd declined because of the phone call with Sean. It was very likely Evan would be with him.

She glanced down at her son and his angry expression. Lily couldn't blame him. If she were in his shoes, she'd be upset, too. "Listen, Evan," she said, taking a seat at the breakfast table. "Can you come sit? I need to talk to you for a minute."

Evan's expression didn't change as he stood there studying her. Finally, he blurted, "Fine. I'll sit."

The implication was there. If she didn't come through with a reasonable explanation, he was out. Lily put her arm around his tension-filled body and rubbed his shoulder. "I got a call last night after you went to bed."

He just stared at her with his lips pressed together as he waited to hear her out.

As much as she didn't want to tell him, didn't want to get his hopes up in case Sean flaked again, she really felt like she just had to be honest. "It was your dad."

Evan's eyes widened with shock and then filled with surprise. "Dad called? Did he want to talk to me? I could've gotten up. I could've—"

"Hold on, bud," she said gently. "He called because he's going to be here and wants to see you over Christmas." She left out the part about Sean demanding two weeks and what day he said he was coming because she wanted to see if she could negotiate a shorter visit with him first. Two weeks was an awfully long time for Evan when he hadn't been in contact with his father for so long.

"He is?" Evan jumped up, his movements jerky with excitement. "When?"

"The details aren't all worked out yet. But that's why I didn't say yes to the trip to Tahoe. We need to finalize plans with your dad first, and if it works out that you still have time for the trip, then we'll change plans."

"Can I tell Mr. Weise that I still might be able to go?" he asked.

"Sure. But remember things are really still up in the air. If he has a hard deadline for the reservation, we won't be able to commit."

Disappointment washed over him as all that excitement

faded. But then he perked up. "Can I call dad today? You know, since he called last night?"

Lily internally groaned. She'd never told him he couldn't call his dad before. Even when Sean had been MIA, Evan had called and left him messages, but Sean never called back. Since his dad was so unresponsive, eventually Evan had given up. If it were Lily in his shoes, she wouldn't want to talk to him at all. But she recognized that her kid was still holding out hope that his dad would show an interest in him. And while she was worried about what damage Sean might do to him, she was glad Evan wasn't so jaded that he wasn't willing to give Sean a chance if he was finally getting his act together. Still, she couldn't have him talking to his dad and making plans until she and Sean came to an understanding. "Maybe tonight. Right now, you need to eat before you go to school."

"Okay." He grinned at her and then threw his arms around her neck. "I love you, Mom."

Lily held on tight and squeezed her eyes shut against the sting of tears. "I love you, too, sweetheart."

"Moooom," he said, rolling his eyes as he pulled away. "Gross. Why can't you just call me Evan like everyone else does?"

She laughed. "Mom's prerogative." She pushed his orange juice toward him and got up to get him some breakfast. "Do you want oatmeal or a bagel?"

"Captain Crunch," he said with a cheeky grin.

She laughed and went to the cabinet where they kept the cereal.

~

LILY SAT at a table in the corner of Love Potions with a cup of coffee and a pastry from the Enchanted Bean Stalk. It was early afternoon, and she was already wishing she could crawl back into bed and pull the covers over her head. The morning rush, combined with orders they were preparing to ship out, had left her back aching and her feet tired. It was going to be a long six more hours until she clocked out. At least at her next job she got to sit down for a few hours.

"Do you mind if I join you?" Chase asked, standing next to the empty chair across from her.

Her lips curved into a small smile. With all the stress in her life, he was the one person who always managed to help ease her anxiety. He was just so… comfortable. "Of course. Did you get the rest of the boxes packed up?"

"They are all packed, labeled, and ready for Lemon when she gets here." Lemon Pepperson owned an express delivery service in town. During the holidays, she offered her services to pick up all the mail-order items from the small businesses in town and made sure they got to the correct shipping services.

"Good." Lily sat back in her chair. "That will make the rest of the afternoon less stressful."

He shrugged. "I have to start working on the orders for tomorrow."

She gave him a sympathetic wrinkle of her nose. "I know it's great for business, but I imagine you're going to need a trip to the spa by the time the season is over."

"I wouldn't mind. How about we go together?" he asked, his eyes twinkling.

Lily glanced down at her plain coffee. "I'd love to, but it's not really in the budget."

"I get it," he said. "Speaking of budgets, I have something for you."

She glanced up at him, curious. "You got me something?"

He nodded. "I have a friend from culinary school whose wife is a lawyer. I sent him an email last night asking if his wife had any resources for you." Chase reached into his pocket and pulled out a piece of paper. "He sent over this number. It's his wife's cousin. She does pro bono family law, and she said to call her and she'll see what she can do."

Lily stared at the piece of paper and then focused on Chase again. "You talked to someone about a lawyer for me?"

"Sort of? I sent an email briefly outlining the situation and asked if they knew of anyone who could help. Is that a problem?"

Lily shook her head slowly. To be honest, she wasn't sure how she felt. Grateful was at the top of the list, but she was also embarrassed for far too many reasons. The fact that she needed a lawyer at all, that she hadn't been the one to go looking for someone, and that she was once again back in a position where she was depending on a man. After she left Sean, she'd vowed to never do that again.

"What is it then? Did you hear from Sean again?" His voice was full of concern.

She sighed. "No. But I had to tell Evan that he called. Now he's excited to see his dad, and I don't want to be the one to take that away from him. I was thinking maybe I should just let Sean see him, and then when Sean gets frustrated by dealing with being a parent for more than two hours, that will be that. And everything will go back to being normal."

Chase leaned forward and took her hand in his. "I can see that logic, but I'd feel better if you called the lawyer. Just to make sure you and Evan are protected."

Ugh. He was right of course. She had to do what was right for Evan even if she didn't want a fight with her ex. Lily nodded. "I will. And thank you. This is above and beyond what anyone else has done for me."

He held her hand tighter and said, "It's not above and beyond. It's what friends do for each other." He leaned forward, kissed her on the cheek, and then disappeared into the back again.

Lily stared at the number and then the clock. Her break was almost over, and customers were starting to file in again. There was no time to call the lawyer. She stuffed the piece of paper in her pocket, gathered her trash, and rushed to get back behind the counter.

"Can I help you?" she asked a lovely woman dressed in a stylish red dress and silver high-heeled boots. She had blond hair that was styled in perfect waves down to her shoulders, and her makeup made her look like she'd just stepped off the pages of a magazine. "What can I get for you?"

The woman gave Lily a dazzling smile. "I need something for my soon-to-be stepson. Something that will win him over." She flashed her left hand, showing off a diamond so big it nearly blinded Lily. "We're going to tell him the news today."

"Congratulations," Lily said, giving the woman a warm smile. "That's exciting for all of you. How old is your fiancé's son?"

"Eight."

Lily nodded. "Okay, does he have a favorite chocolate or candy?"

She shrugged. "I don't know. My fiancé said something about chocolate mint."

"Perfect. My son loved chocolate mint when he was younger, too. He couldn't get enough of those thin mint wafers. We have a holiday box of those if you like, or I can put together a gift bag of different items that include mint chocolates, hot cocoa, caramel squares, that type of thing."

"Let's just go with the mint wafers," the woman said. "If that's his favorite, then I'd rather go overboard."

"Sure thing." Lily packaged up the candy, gift wrapped it, and waved as the woman left.

Lily stared after her, remembering what it was like to have time and money to look that good. Before the divorce, she'd been stylish too. But one good thing that had come with leaving Sean was the realization of just how unhappy she'd been with him. Knowing what she knew now, she'd still leave him, only she'd have made an effort to leave him sooner. She deserved better, and no amount of makeup, hair appointments, or shopping trips were enough to cover up the fact that she'd been suffocating in that marriage.

It might be harder to make ends meet, but she didn't care. Her freedom to be herself and to raise her son in a loving environment was all she needed.

CHAPTER FIFTEEN

$\mathcal{L}$ily was just getting ready to help Chase with a batch of cupcakes for the shop when she heard the front door chime and a familiar voice called out, "Mom! Guess what grandpa and I got."

She poked her head around the corner and spotted Evan with her dad, Ben, standing in the middle of the empty shop, each of them holding a handful of shopping bags.

"Hmm, socks?" Lily asked as she walked over and pulled an empty tray out of the front case to restock with chocolate-covered caramels

Evan rolled his eyes. "No. Why would we get socks? Those are boring."

"So your toes don't freeze?" she asked.

"Guess again," Evan ordered.

Ben grimaced at Lily, making her believe that she wasn't going to be thrilled with the answer.

"Is it a Christmas gift?" Lily asked, eyeing him.

"Yes, of course," Evan said.

Lily glanced over at Chase, who was standing in the

doorway. He looked curious as he watched the exchange, and she wondered if her son had purchased something for him. "Who's it for?" she asked Evan

"That's what I want you to guess." He bounced on the balls of his feet.

"Well, I'm guessing it's not for gramps, since you were with him. Or me."

"Nope. Keep trying."

"Vin?"

He shook his head.

She went through a few more names of kids in his class before she finally asked, "Chase?"

Evan's cheeks turned pink as if he were embarrassed, but he shook his head.

"Okay. I give. Who's it for?"

He pulled a small box out of one of his bags and handed it to her. As soon as she saw it, she had to swallow a groan. It was a tie pin that had a Christmas tree and Christmas Grove engraved on it. There was only one person he'd think to get a gift like that for.

Sean.

Evan's father had a tie pin collection and always use to tell Evan that, once he was grown and had a high-powered job of his own, he'd pass them on to him.

"Looks like this is for your dad," she said, trying to muster some enthusiasm. "That's very thoughtful of you, Evan."

"He'll like it, right?" Evan asked.

Lily doubted it. He wasn't likely to wear a Christmas themed pin and certainly not one from Christmas Grove. Sean would likely sneer at the town and its festivities. He was more of a city guy. "I'm sure he'll love anything you get him, Ev."

Evan grinned and put the present back in the bag.

Lily cleared her throat. "What else have you two been up to? Did you get all your shopping done?"

"Mostly," her dad said. "I need to get a dozen cupcakes for the card players tomorrow."

Lily glanced at the case, noting there were only two left. "We're almost out."

"I'm just getting ready to make more," Chase said. "If you want to wait or come back just before closing, I'll have them ready for you."

Ben looked at his watch. "I've got to pick up a package at the post office. I can come back."

"Can I stay here?" Evan asked, his eyes pleading with Lily.

She knew he hated waiting in line at the post office. "I still have about an hour. Do you think you can entertain yourself for that long?"

"He can help me," Chase said. "I could use an assistant while I work on the cupcakes."

Lily glanced over at Mrs. Pottson, who was sitting at the desk doing paperwork. "Is that okay? Do you mind if Evan helps out?"

"Not at all," Mrs. Pottson said without looking up. "My daughter was always in here with me while she was growing up." She glanced over at Chase. "Just keep an eye on him. Make sure he's not using the heavy-duty mixer or messing with the ovens."

"Will do, boss." Chase gestured to Evan. "Come on. Get back here and wash your hands. Then we'll get an apron on you."

Evan followed Chase into the back room, while Lily joined her father at the table.

"I guess you heard about Sean," Lily said.

"Only what Evan told me, which wasn't much. Care to fill me in?" he asked, his expression worried.

She told him about the phone call and how Chase had found a lawyer who was willing to work pro bono.

"Chase is right. You need to call that lawyer," her father said.

"But what if that just exacerbates everything?" Lily asked. "You know how Sean is. The harder I fight, the more he's going to dig in."

"Lily, my love, I know you hate conflict, especially conflict with Sean, but you have to do this for Evan. You can't let Sean disrupt his life. We don't know what kind of damage he's going to cause."

She sucked in a long breath. "I know. I just… I don't want a huge fight like we had during the divorce. Especially if he's going to ghost us again."

"Sometimes you just have to do what you have to do," Ben said as he got up. "Call the lawyer. Even if it's just as a precaution. I have to head to the post office now. I'll be back."

Lily stood and kissed her dad on the cheek. "Love you, Dad."

"Love you, too, Pumpkin."

When the door chimed after Ben left, Mrs. Pottson stared after him and said, "Your dad is a good-looking man."

Lily let out a huff of laughter. "If you say so."

"I do. Did he say something about playing cards?" she asked.

"Yeah. He plays at the bingo hall with his buddies once a week," Lily confirmed.

"Interesting." Mrs. Pottson patted her hair into place and stuck one of her hips out in an exaggerated pose. "Maybe I'll take them a little something tomorrow. You know, add a little holiday cheer."

Lily snickered. "I'm sure they'd all love that, considering most of them are widowers."

"Hmm, even better," she said. "Nothing like having some choices for a New Year's Eve date." She winked at Lily and then went back to her computer. It wasn't long before she packed up and said her goodbyes. "I'll be by in the morning for a gift box. See you then."

Lily waved at her and went back to restocking the display case. She listened as Chase and Evan bantered about baking in the next room. Evan was quizzing him about ingredients in different types of pastries, while Chase challenged him on cooking times and temperatures. Lily chuckled to herself. Who would've guessed the man she was dating and her kid would be geeking out over recipes? It was quite possibly the most heartwarming moment she'd experienced recently.

The door chimes caught her attention, and Lily glanced up to find the same gorgeous blond with the perfect hair and makeup from earlier in the day walking in. There was a man behind her, but the woman was blocking him.

"Did you forget something?" Lily asked with a smile.

The woman returned the smile with a tentative one. "Um, no, not exactly." She took a step to the side, and Lily let out a gasp of surprise when she spotted the tall, slightly overweight man she used to be married to.

"Hello, Lily," Sean said, running a hand through his wavy blond hair. He flashed that charming smile of his and added, "It's good to see you."

She glanced through the door where Chase and Evan were busy filling cupcake tins. Neither had noticed the new visitor.

Lily rushed to get out from behind the counter and said,

"Sean, what are you doing here?"

"Melissa and I are on our way to Tahoe for a quick getaway. I thought we'd stop by to say hi to Evan. I called, but you didn't answer your phone," he said casually with a bright smile as if he hadn't called her the night before to threaten her.

"You can't just stop in like this," she hissed.

He blinked and jerked back. "You're really upset that I stopped by to see my son?"

"What do you think?" she asked through clenched teeth. Her entire body was shaking with fury. "You can't just do whatever you want, whenever you want. Not after—"

"Dad!" Evan came running out of the back room, his arms open wide, and crashed into Sean, clutching him so hard that he nearly knocked Sean over.

Sean let out a chuckle and returned the hug, pressing one hand on the back of Evan's head while the other patted his back. "Hello, son," Sean said gruffly, emotion clogging his throat. "I've missed you so much."

"I've missed you, too," Evan said, his voice thick with tears.

Lily was so conflicted. On the one hand, she wanted to scream. Wanted to throw Sean out and tell him to never come back after the way he'd abandoned his kid. At the same time, Evan didn't deserve to be hurt because his father was a jerk. She backed up and leaned against the counter just to have something to hold onto.

"I'm so sorry we just stopped in like this," Melissa whispered to her. "It's just that I've heard so much about Evan, and I really wanted to meet him."

Lily stared at the other woman. She'd honestly forgotten that she was even there. Then she spotted the bag she'd handed her earlier with the mint chocolate wafers. Hadn't she said they were for her soon-to-be stepson? Her *eight-year-old* stepson? Bile rose in the back of Lily's throat. It seemed clear that the gift had been for Evan despite the age issue, and this woman was going to be his stepmother. She couldn't help wondering if Melissa got his age wrong or if it had been Sean. Evan was eight when Sean had last seen him.

"A heads-up would've been nice," Lily choked out.

"I didn't realize you were Evan's mom when I was in earlier. I'm so sorry, otherwise I would've said something then," Melissa said, reaching out to grab Lily's hand.

Lily stepped away and put her hands behind her back. It was childish, but she didn't care. These two had completely blindsided her.

"I meant from Evan's father," Lily said without looking at her.

Sean lifted his gaze and narrowed his eyes at Lily. It was a warning to not cause a scene. Had Evan not been there, Lily would've caused the biggest scene any of them had ever witnessed. This was completely unacceptable.

"We'd like to take Evan to dinner," Sean told Lily. Then he glanced down at Evan. "What do you say, son? Do you have a few hours for your good old dad?"

Evan nodded. "Always." His face was streaked with tears, and Lily's heart splintered. "Is it okay, Mom? I only have a little bit of homework. I can do it when I get home."

She couldn't say no. She couldn't take this away from him. Sean had finally walked back into his life, and while she hated her ex for the way he'd done it, she also couldn't deprive her child of his father. Lily sucked in a deep breath and nodded. She glared at Sean over Evan's head when she said, "Don't keep him out too late. Seven at the latest. He has school tomorrow."

Sean smiled at her pleasantly, obviously pleased he'd won that round. "I'll have Evan home at seven and not a minute later. Besides we're still driving up to Tahoe tonight. I just wanted him to meet Melissa before our upcoming trip together."

"Can I speak to you privately for a moment?" Lily asked, her voice shaking. She could not have her ex talking about some trip he had planned before she okayed whatever they were planning to do.

Sean glanced at his watch and shook his head. "I was going to take Evan shopping before dinner. We really don't have time."

"You have time," Lily insisted. "We'll talk now, or there won't be a dinner."

"Mom!" Evan cried. "Stop being like that. Dad just wants to see me."

"I know, Evan. I'm not saying no. I just need to discuss a few things with your father first."

Melissa slipped her arm through Sean's and whispered to him. "Maybe you should talk to her for a moment. She *is* his mother."

Sean's features softened as he looked at her. Then he nodded. "Sure, love. We'll just be a moment."

Lily glanced over her shoulder at Chase, who was still standing in the doorway that led to the back of the shop. "Can you keep an eye on Evan and the shop for a minute?"

He nodded. "Of course."

"Thanks." She gestured to Sean and stalked outside. The moment they were on the sidewalk, she turned on him. "What do you think you're doing?"

"I have a right to see my son, Lily," he said, crossing his arms over his chest.

"It's rich what you think you have a right to do after being MIA for three years and not even contributing any financial support for your son. You have no idea what you've done to Evan, do you?" she barked.

He glanced into the shop at his son, who was sitting at a table and opening the gift from Melissa. When he turned back to Lily, he said, "You have no idea what I've been through. Losing my family really did a number on me, Lily. I'm just now getting back to myself, and I want to repair the damage I've done to my relationship with Evan. Would you really deny me that right?"

His words managed to instill some sympathy in her, and the moment she recognized it, she wanted to scream. He didn't deserve her understanding. If that's what he needed, he'd have to find it somewhere else. "You don't get to talk about how hard things have been. Not to me."

Sean glanced away, and it was the first time she'd ever seen him uncomfortable when they'd discussed their split. "I just want to spend time with my son. Is that a bad thing?"

"No. But you don't get to dictate to me when you do it," she said.

"It's just dinner, Lily," he said, sounding exasperated.

"It's not just dinner. It's two weeks over Christmas, which you didn't *ask* me about. You just *demanded* that time, like I'm supposed to just let you do whatever you want with Evan when you don't even know him now. Where is this vacation? Who is it with? And why should I say yes?"

He clenched his teeth together as his hands fisted. She knew he wanted to scream at her. He'd done it before, but this time he kept himself in check. "I've purchased a vacation home in Lake Tahoe with Melissa. We're getting it set up this week, and on Saturday, I'll come back to pick up Evan. It's just me and her until right before Christmas when her family comes in. I want Evan to meet them. We'll be skiing and sledding and doing all the winter things. He'll just be a few hours away, and then I'll bring him home on New Year's Day. If all goes well, I want to work out a visitation schedule."

Lily felt like she'd been sucker-punched. He'd purchased a vacation home in Lake Tahoe while never once paying a dime in child support? "You've got to be kidding me."

"About what?" he asked.

"A vacation home? You owe me three years of child support, and you bought a vacation home?" she asked, her eyes wide with disbelief. "And now you want a visitation schedule?"

"I'm trying to do the right thing, Lily! What more do you want from me? Money? Is that what this is about? I always knew that was why you married me."

"What?" she ground out. "What did you just say?"

"You heard me. Fine. I'll cut you a check when I drop Evan off. But right now, I'm taking my son to dinner. If you try to stop me, you'll have a legal battle the size of Texas on your hands. I've seen your house and have pictures of you and that man making out in public. How do you think that will look to a judge compared to me and Melissa? I can give him the best of everything, while you have him working in a potion shop after school. Think about it, Lily."

He didn't wait for her response as he strode back into the shop and held his arms out for Evan.

She walked back into the store, placed her hand on Evan's shoulder, and said, "Go have dinner with your dad. We'll talk when you get home."

"Thanks, Mom." He gave her a quick hug before following his dad and future stepmom out the door.

As soon as they were gone, Chase asked, "Are you okay?"

"No." She pulled the piece of paper with the lawyer's phone number out of her pocket and dialed.

CHAPTER SIXTEEN

"How did it go?" Chase asked as he cleaned up his work area.

Lily stood in the doorway, still clutching her phone. There were circles under her eyes, and she looked like she hadn't slept in days. It was obvious that the interaction with her ex had really sucked the energy right out of her. "It went okay. She asked me to send our custody agreement over so she'll have it on record, and then she's going to write an amendment agreement to send to his lawyer before he takes Evan to Tahoe."

"What's in the amendment?" Chase asked.

"Just stuff like how far in advance he needs to make arrangements to see Evan so that he can't just call and demand we change our plans. And if he's relocating, then we should set up a visitation schedule. She also wants to go after him for child support, but I don't want to do that until after the visit."

"Why not?" Chase asked, though he figured he already knew the answer.

"He said he'd pay me when he drops Evan off after the trip.

But I won't believe that until I see it. Mostly, I just don't want to mess up the holiday for Evan." She pressed a hand to her forehead. "You saw how excited Evan was when he saw his father. I can't take that away from him."

Chase nodded, though he was uneasy about the entire situation. He hated the way Sean treated them both and had doubts that the man had Evan's best interest at heart. But Chase couldn't say any of that. He was the newcomer to the picture and had to trust Lily's judgment. He had no reason not to. She was a wonderful mother.

Lily turned and bumped into a tray on the counter, causing a fresh batch of pecan clusters to scatter all over the floor. "Ugh! I'm going to be a nervous wreck until Sean drops Evan off."

Chase hurried over to help her. "It's okay. It happens."

"I know, but..." She pressed a hand to her heart. "I'm just stressed."

"I know." He took the remaining chocolates from her hands and said, "Why don't you let me distract you while Evan is out with Sean? We could go to the holiday festival in the square."

She let out an exaggerated sigh. "That sounds lovely, but I told Mr. Fredrick that I'd spend a little time working on the books over at his train store. Ever since he opened his brick-and-mortar store a few months ago, he's needed some help keeping things organized."

Disappointment wound through Chase, but he shoved it down. Now wasn't the time to be thinking about his needs. All he wanted to do was lift Lily's spirits. "Okay. I'll walk you over there. I was going to look for a new train car for my set anyway."

Lily nodded. "Okay."

They finished cleaning up the shop, and after Chase locked

up, they turned in the direction of the train store. It was only a few blocks down, making Chase wish it was further just so he could spend more time with Lily.

"Ohmigod. Look," Lily said, pointing toward a freestanding mailbox near the corner of the street.

Chase glanced over and grinned when he spotted a reindeer wearing a Santa hat on his antlers crossing the road. "Looks like he has a friend with him." Chase nodded toward the smaller reindeer behind him.

Lily let out a delighted laugh. "Look, he has a red nose!"

Chase took a moment to appreciate that her mood had shifted. She'd been so upset after the altercation with her ex, and rightfully so. But now, she'd found a way to set that aside and enjoy a little bit of what Christmas Grove had to offer. Squinting, Chase took a step forward, searching for signs the reindeer was indeed a Rudolph lookalike. He frowned and squinted harder. "What am I missing? I don't see a red nose."

"Just kidding," Lily said, her voice tinged with laughter. "But I'm always on the lookout this time of year."

Chase grinned at her, loving her playful side. "Do you keep an eye out for Frosty as well?"

"Of course," she said, sounding kind of offended. "Doesn't everyone?"

"I used to until that one year I found a top hat, a button, and a corn cob pipe in a puddle of water in my yard."

Lily snickered. "What happened to the coal?"

He shrugged. "Hard to say. But from that point on, I figured Frosty had succumbed to global warming."

She threw her head back and laughed.

Chase chuckled, loving that he'd lifted her spirits. "But if you're up to it, we can build another snowman and see if his spirit is still alive."

"I'd love that." Lily grabbed his arm and leaned into him. "Thank you, Chase."

He smiled down at her. "For what?"

"For just being you. For being a friend when I needed one." She laid her head on his shoulder and squeezed his arm in a warm gesture. "Today has been... *awful* for the most part, but you're a bright spot. I just wanted you to know."

He kissed the top of her head and whispered, "Anytime."

A few minutes later, Chase pulled the door open and followed Lily into Saint Nick's Locomotives.

Nick Fredrick glanced up from his spot behind the counter and smiled warmly at Lily. "There you are. I was waiting for you."

"I'm sorry, Mr. Fredrick. Am I late? It's been one heck of a day."

"Late? Oh no. I have something for you." He waved for her to join him behind the counter.

She turned to Chase. "Thanks again for today. You have no idea how much you helped."

He squeezed her hand and said, "I only wish I could've done more."

Lily gave him a quick hug and said she'd see him tomorrow and then hurried behind the counter to talk to the shop owner.

Chase took his time looking at the trains on display. He hadn't really been intending to add anything to his collection that his dad had given him. But he did have something else in mind. After checking out a bunch of different options, he finally landed on the Holiday Express HO train set. He placed it on the counter and waited until Mr. Fredrick returned to ring him up.

"Oh, this is a lovely one. It will look really good under your tree," Mr. Fredrick said.

"That's what I thought." Chase paid the man and was just getting ready to leave the store when Lily appeared again.

Her eyes were red rimmed as if she'd been crying, but she was smiling at Mr. Fredrick when she said, "Thank you again. You have no idea what this means to me."

"You deserve it, Lily. You work too hard. Now go get yourself something nice, and I'll see you after the new year." He patted her shoulder and pulled out a set of keys. "You two go on," he said, gesturing to her and Chase. "I've got eggnog waiting for me at home."

Lily turned to Chase. "If you're still available, I'd like to take you up on that offer to check out the holiday festival."

"I'm definitely still available." Chase held his hand out. When she took it, he led her back outside where a light dusting of snow had just started to fall.

She glanced at the bag he was holding. "Whatcha got there?"

"A holiday train set. I couldn't resist," he said.

"Mr. Fredrick stocks some really nice ones. I hope it goes well with the rest of your collection."

Chase shrugged one shoulder. "I'm not worried about that."

Lily lifted her face and opened her mouth, catching a tiny snowflake.

Chase watched her, his heart swelling with affection. He loved the way she still found joy in life even when her ex was causing turmoil. "How do you do that?"

"Do what?" she asked, tilting her head to the side. "Catch snowflakes?"

"No." He chuckled. "How do you compartmentalize what's happening in your life? I know you haven't just brushed aside the fight with your ex. I know you're still fuming on the inside.

But you're also here, enjoying the snowfall. Most people aren't great at that sort of thing."

She pressed her lips together into a thin line as she contemplated his question. "I guess it's because after I left Sean, he was so awful to me that one day I decided I wasn't going to let him steal my joy anymore. Do I hate what he's doing? Yes. Am I going to keep Evan from him? No, not unless he does something to prove he's an unsafe parent. For all his faults, that's never been the case. Evan's relationship with him is different than the one I have. I don't ever want to be that parent who puts her kid in the middle. So for tonight, even though I'm mad as hell, I'm choosing to believe the best in Sean and that he really does just want to see his son." She forced a bright smile onto her face. "Meanwhile, I'm going to let you distract me so that I don't fall into a pit of resentment."

"You're amazing, you know that?"

"I'm just trying to muddle through," she said modestly. Then she glanced up at him with vulnerable eyes. "Can we not talk about it anymore? Not now anyway. I just need to get through the next couple of hours, and I'd rather do it without thinking about my ex."

"Of course." He squeezed her hand and said, "So, Mr. Fredrick didn't need you tonight after all?"

She shook her head. "He said he's already caught up on the books. He decided last minute to go to Florida to visit his sister for the holidays and is closing for the rest of the month. Which means I don't have to be back until January." Her expression turned to one of pure disbelief when she added in a whisper, "He's giving me paid leave, and he gave me a bonus for the year. A really nice bonus."

"That's great. I'm sure you deserve every cent," Chase said as they walked back up Main Street toward the town square.

"I don't know about that, but I'm grateful all the same."

She's everything I never knew I needed, Chase thought. His deceased wife would've answered his statement very differently. He was ninety-five percent certain she'd have complained that it should've been more. Which may or may not have been true, but it took months of living on his own to realize just how much negativity there'd been in their marriage toward the end. It was refreshing to be around someone who found the positive in most situations.

"Are you hungry?" Chase asked her. "There's a great food truck up here. Have you had their cranberry and brie turnovers?"

Lily shook her head. "No, we rarely eat out. But those sound amazing."

"We have to get them then." Chase strode over to the food truck and ordered the turnovers as well as two cups of eggnog. When he returned, he handed her the eggnog and a paper tray holding the food.

"These smell wonderful," Lily said.

Chase took a sip of the eggnog and let out a small moan of pleasure. "This is delicious."

Lily led them over to a small sidewalk table where they sat and ate. When she bit into her first turnover, her eyes rolled into the back of her head, and Chase wanted to find a way to illicit that response over and over again. There wasn't anything better than the expression on her face when something brought her pleasure.

"Why are you looking at me like that?" Lily asked.

He cleared his throat. "I've never seen anyone lovelier than you."

Lily let out a huff of laughter. "I don't know why you're trying to flatter me, Chase Garland, but after the last twenty-four hours, I'll take it. Thank you. Between your compliments and these cranberry brie turnovers, I think I'm more than a little spoiled."

"If this is spoiling you, then get used to it. I'm planning on a lot more of this over the next few months."

Her cheeks flushed pink as she gave him a shy smile. Then she said, "Only months?"

He chuckled. "It's up for debate."

"Good."

When they were finished, Chase dropped his purchase off in his SUV that was still parked near Love Potions, and then they walked hand-in-hand to the town square. The twenty-foot tree glowed in the center while white doves trimmed the tree with red ribbons. A musicianless string quartet magically played classical Christmas music, and enchanted snowmen spun around on the dance floor.

"Looks like Frosty might've survived global warming after all," Lily said.

"Those are fake Frostys whose hours are numbered," he joked.

"I don't even think they are made totally of snow," Lily mused. "They are animated costumes that are covered in a layer of snow."

"That's not right at all," Chase said as he steered her away from the vendors and the dance floor.

"Right? It's cheating in my opinion."

Chase chuckled. "How do you feel about Christmas movies?"

"Christmas movies?" she asked curiously. "I like them. Though I haven't had time to sit down and watch any yet this season. Evan isn't into them. If I put one on, he starts getting antsy after about ten minutes and then forget it. He'll ask me a million questions about something else and the next thing I know, the credits are rolling. So I usually watch them after he goes to bed. But lately I've been too exhausted to watch anything. I've been reading instead."

His lips twitched in amusement. That was far more information than he needed, but he loved that she always explained herself. He felt like he was really getting to know her. "Okay, how about now?" He gestured to a grassy field that had a large screen set up. There was a sign indicating that they were playing *A Spellbound Christmas*.

Lily glanced around at the people sitting on blankets in the grass. "Do we get a blanket?"

"Of course you do," Mrs. Pottson said, seemingly appearing out of nowhere. She snapped her fingers, and a green velvet blanket materialized in the air in front of Lily. It floated down slowly and landed softly in her arms. "When you're done, snap your own fingers three times and it will vanish."

"Thank you," Lily said and eyed her boss. "Are you in charge of the Christmas festival this year?"

"In charge? No. Just helping out." Mrs. Pottson waved, and just like that she was gone again.

"Wow. Looks like this town is pulling out all the stops this year," Chase said.

Lily nodded. "It sure makes me appreciate living here. Ever since we arrived, it's just felt like home."

Chase nodded, "I felt the same." He spread the blanket, and they sat next to each other with their hands nearly touching. "If you think about it, one could say maybe our story is just like one of these holiday movies."

"You think?" Lily turned to stare at him, her eyes twinkling in amusement. "Are you saying one of us is going to be offered a job in the big city, and then decide to take it, even though our heart is here in this town and belongs to someone else?"

He laughed. "Sure. Or one of us is a baker who's going to enter a baking contest for prize money to save the local dog shelter. And in the end, we wind up together with a new puppy and a renewed faith in Christmas."

"Well, you're the baker. So I guess that's on you. As for the puppy... I'm not sure I'm really in the market for one," she said.

"You say that now, but just wait until you see those sweet puppy-dog eyes. You'll be a goner," he teased.

Lily leaned into him, laughing. "There are no truer words." She pointed a finger at him and squinted with one eye. "Don't you go getting any ideas, now. No puppies for Christmas."

"New Year's then?"

She rolled her eyes and was just about to turn her attention to the movie when her phone buzzed. She frowned as she quickly answered it. "Sean? What's wrong?"

CHAPTER SEVENTEEN

"Where the hell are you?" Sean demanded.

Lily's blood pressure spiked. "At the Christmas festival. Where are you? Where's Evan? Is he okay?"

"Of course he's okay. He's currently sitting on your front porch, waiting to get in." Sean's voice was full of anger and impatience. "Are you with your boy toy again? When were you planning to come home? What if we'd just dropped him off and left? My son would be waiting for who knows how long out in the cold."

"You said you'd have him home at seven, Sean. It's barely six," she said, pushing herself up onto her feet. "What happened?"

"Nothing happened. We had dinner, it's over, and now Melissa and I want to get on the road. But we obviously can't do that since you're not here, which blows my mind after that tantrum you had earlier. I'd have thought you'd be waiting at home with bated breath to make sure Evan didn't have a hair out of place the moment I dropped him off. Instead, you're out at the Christmas festival, doing what? Drinking spiked eggnog and dancing around like a teenager?"

Lily pulled the phone away from her ear and blinked at it. Was this real life? Had he really just insulted her for going to the town Christmas festival? "I'll be there in less than ten minutes. Surely you can wait that long."

"Just hurry up. Melissa is eager to get on the road."

Lily slammed her finger down on the End button, nearly knocking the phone out of her hand.

"What's wrong?" Chase asked, already standing with the blanket folded and in his arms.

"It was Sean. They're already at my house, and Evan doesn't seem to have his house key. I'm sorry, Chase. But I have to go." She turned and started to jog back toward her car, leaving him in the field.

LILY MADE it home in eight minutes. She might have run a red light and broken some speeding laws, but no one pulled her over, so luck was on her side. When she pulled into her driveway, Sean jumped out of a fancy Cadillac Escalade and stalked toward her, while Melissa sat with Evan on the front porch. They appeared to be going through a book together.

Sean caught up with her while they were still out of earshot from their son and his fiancée. Her ex grabbed her arm, stopping her. "We need to talk."

Lily jerked away from him. "Don't put your hands on me, Sean. I'm not your property."

"Fine." He held his hands up in a surrender motion. "No need to get touchy about it. For crying out loud, Lily, I just wanted to talk to you for a minute."

"About what?" She crossed her arms over her chest and glared at him.

"You know what it's about. I can't believe you're already calling a lawyer when all I want to do is see my son. Are you really that bitter?" He shook his head, a sad expression on his face. "It's been years, Lily. Do we really need to keep doing this to each other? I've moved on. And apparently, so have you. Though I'd appreciate it if you didn't leave my son in his care."

Lily glanced over at Melissa. "But your fiancée is acceptable?"

"Are you engaged to this man you're sleeping with?" he asked coldly.

"I'm not talking about this with you." She started to move away but when he spoke again, she stopped in her tracks.

"If you don't call off your lawyer, I'll file for full custody."

Lily turned around and wondered how she'd ever thought she loved this man. As much as she hated the thought of putting Evan through a custody dispute, she knew she couldn't bow down to his demands. She wasn't asking for anything unreasonable. All she wanted was some stability in their lives. "All I want is a formal visitation schedule. It's not fair to either me or Evan for you to dictate when you want to see him. If you can't handle that, then I guess we'll go back to court."

"Court?" Melissa asked.

Lily spun to find his fiancée standing right behind her. The woman's eyes were wide, and she looked alarmed.

"It's nothing, Mel," Sean said with an easygoing smile. All traces of his anger and resentment had vanished. "Lily's just a little upset about our last-minute planning. It's nothing we need to take to court, right, Lily? I'll be better about communication from now on."

"Oh, it's my fault," Melissa said, pressing one hand to her

chest and reaching out to squeeze Lily's hand with her other one. "I've just heard so much about Evan and couldn't wait to meet him. I'm the one who suggested we stop by on the way. I'm sorry if we interrupted any plans."

The woman seemed so sincere that Lily wasn't even sure what to say. Finally she just shook her head. "You didn't interrupt anything important. I'd just like some advanced warning about visits and vacations so that we can be sure they work for Evan's schedule."

"Of course," Melissa said earnestly. "I told Sean to call about the Tahoe trip earlier, but he wanted the sale on the property to close before he got Evan's hopes up. We'll be better about working together as a team going forward." Melissa dropped Lily's hand. And then to Lily's horror, she flung her arms around Lily, squeezing her tightly. "Sean has spoken so highly of you. I just know we're going to be great friends."

Lily was shocked into silence. Her ex had spoken highly of her? When? And why hadn't this woman noticed that Sean hadn't been in their lives at all for the past three years?

Melissa waved at Evan and climbed into Sean's fancy SUV.

Lily glanced at Sean. "What's really going on here?"

"I don't know what you're talking about, Lily. There's nothing going on except the fact that I want to have time with my son. And since Melissa is going to be my wife, she wants to get to know him, too. That's all. But if you're going to try to railroad me with a lawyer, then you'd better be prepared for the fight. Because as I've told my wife-to-be, I'll do anything for my son."

More like you'd do anything to win, Lily thought.

"I'll be back Saturday at ten. Make sure Evan's ready." Sean strode up to the porch, stretched his arms out wide, and stood there while Evan flung himself at his father. They hugged for a long moment before Sean let him go. Her ex didn't say anything as he brushed past her to his SUV.

Lily watched him get into his vehicle and stood there until the taillights faded in the distance.

"Mom?" Evan asked tentatively.

"Yeah, baby?" She turned to see her son standing next to her.

"I'm cold."

"Me, too. Let's get inside." She held his hand in hers, and together they went into her small house.

Evan ran to the kitchen to get something to drink while Lily sat on her couch wondering what to do next. She didn't want a legal battle on her hands. But she couldn't sit around and let her ex call the shots in their lives.

Her son's footsteps caught her attention as the wood floors creaked. She glanced at him to find him holding two mugs of hot cocoa. He handed her one and sat next to her on the couch.

"Are you okay?" she asked him.

"Yeah."

Lily nodded. "How was the visit?"

He shrugged. "Weird. Melissa is nice, but dad was weird."

"How so?" Lily turned sideways on the couch to give him her full attention.

"I don't know. He was on the phone a lot, but when he wasn't, he spent most of his time talking about things we used to do together. Only they were things I did with you or with my friends' families, not with Dad."

Lily frowned. "Like what?"

He chewed on his lower lip. "I don't know. He talked about a trip to the beach, but I only remember going with you that one time and then again with Benji and his family. He mentioned the fair that came to town, but dad wasn't there. I can remember waiting for him to come home, but he didn't, so you took me. Stuff like that."

Lily's heart nearly broke. There were so many times when Sean had disappointed her son. Evan was right of course. Sean hadn't been there for the beach or the fair. Or the trip to Six Flags, or when they went to pick out Christmas trees, or when Evan tried ice skating for the first time. He'd missed so much, and Lily had always thought it was for work. It turned out it wasn't. He'd been having an affair and sacrificed not just his marriage, but also spending time with Evan.

"I don't know what to say about that, baby. I suspect he regrets missing out on those days. Maybe what he says is true, and he really does want to make up for lost time." Even as the words came out of her mouth, she didn't believe them. She'd bet her entire month's salary that Sean would find a way to let Evan down again. And that's why she couldn't just make nice with her ex and forget the lawyers. No matter how much he threatened her, she wasn't going to roll over and let him call the shots. Not when Evan's heart was on the line.

"You really think so?" Evan asked, his expression somewhat guarded, but she didn't miss the spark of hope in his tone.

Lily wrapped her arm around his shoulders and pulled him in for a hug. "I'm not sure what he's thinking, but I really hope so."

"Me, too." He laid his head on her shoulder.

They sat there, staring at the tree until finally Lily asked, "Do you have any homework to do?"

"Just a few math problems."

She reluctantly pulled away and gently nudged him. "better get those done. It's getting late."

He nodded, and for once he didn't try to stall before getting to his feet and climbing the stairs.

Lily stared after him until her phone pinged with a text. It was Chase.

Everything okay?

Lily felt tears sting her eyes, but she blinked them away. She hadn't ever had someone like Chase in her corner. It was both comforting and disconcerting. She quickly tapped out a response. *It is now.*

Good. See you tomorrow?

Lily sucked in a deep breath and hit the Call button.

"Hey, what's up?" Chase asked.

"Are you free for dinner tomorrow night?" she asked.

"With you?"

"Me and Evan. I'm cooking." Her heart was nearly pounding right out of her chest. She'd never asked a man out before, and certainly not for dinner with her kid.

"Then absolutely." There was a smile in his tone that put Lily at ease. "Can I bring anything?"

Lily felt the tension ease from her shoulders. "Dessert?"

"I'm on it." There was a pause, and then he added, "Lily?"

"Yeah?"

His tone was gentle when he said, "Thanks for inviting me."

Her heart swelled, and Lily knew then that she was all in.

CHAPTER EIGHTEEN

*C*hase didn't intend to go out that evening when he needed to be at work at six in the morning. But when he'd run into Zach and Rex at the gas station, they'd insisted he join them for a drink at Sleighed, the local pub. He'd gone out to pick up a few ingredients to make the dessert he'd promised Lily. But instead, he was sitting across from his two buddies while they toasted to a night out on the town.

"Get in on this, Chase," Zach said, holding a beer bottle up. "To guys' night."

Chase clinked bottles with them and echoed, "To guys' night."

They all took long swigs of their beers and then slammed them back down on the table.

"It's been way too long," Rex said.

"Way too long since what?" Chase asked.

"Since we've been out for guys' night," Zach volunteered. "You'll see soon enough."

Chase gave him a side-eye glance. "What does that mean?"

The two other men gave each other a look and then started

laughing. Rex ran a hand over his light brown hair and sat back in his chair. "Don't think we didn't notice how close you're getting to that pretty blonde you work with at Love Potions."

Chase clutched his beer, not sure what to say. They were officially dating, but he doubted Lily wanted him to spread their business around town. On the other hand, the two men who were sitting across from him were married to Lily's friends. These weren't strangers.

"So," Zach prompted, "how's it going with Lily?"

"Good," Chase said and downed more of his beer.

They both chuckled.

"Okay, man. We get it," Rex offered. "But just know we're all pretty protective of Lily and Evan, so if you're not serious, then—"

"It's serious," Chase said, both amused and slightly annoyed that he was getting *the talk* from his friend.

"Did you hear that, Rex?" Zach asked. "It's serious."

"I heard," Rex said. "Now drop it before he decks both of us."

"Fine. How about we order some wings?" Zach got up. "I'll get us another round of beers, too."

Chase watched him go and wondered how long he had to stay before he could make his excuses and go home. It wasn't that he didn't want to spend time with Zach and Rex, it was that he'd promised Lily dessert and wanted to make her something special.

"Hey, isn't that Olivia?" Rex asked.

"Zach's friend?" Chase asked, following his gaze. The tall, raven-haired beauty was stunning in a sweater dress, leggings, and knee-high boots. Her hair was swept up on top of her head with a few locks framing her face.

"That's her. Looks like she's on a date."

Chase eyed them, noting how stiff Olivia looked as her date guided her toward them. He was tall, dressed in ripped jeans, and wore a backward cap. It didn't look like he'd put much effort into his appearance, and it made Chase shake his head.

"Hey, Olivia," Rex said as they passed.

She waved and gave him a wide-eyed look that Chase thought for sure meant she was silently asking for help.

"Looks like a blind date," Chase said, recognizing the discomfort. He'd been on a few himself after he lost his wife and vowed never, ever again.

"It really does." Rex nodded toward them. "Looks like he isn't scoring any points."

Her date had his face in his phone and was busy texting nonstop.

They had a small exchange before her date scowled and went back to texting. A moment later, he got up abruptly and stalked out of the pub. Olivia threw some money on the table and then hightailed it over to them.

Zach arrived at the same time with the wings and more beer.

"Thank the gods you guys are here," Olivia said, taking a seat between Chase and Zach. "Do you think that was the world record for shortest dates?"

"What happened?" Zach asked her and then smirked. "What did you do to scare him off? Reveal your fetish for furries?"

"Oh not this again," she said, laughing. She turned to Chase and added, "I don't have a furry fetish. That's Zach's thing."

The pair cracked up at their inside joke. When Olivia sobered, she said, "I didn't do anything. The man was distracted from the time we met outside right up until he abruptly left, muttering something about how he didn't have time to deal with idiots."

Zach's expression turned stormy. "He called you an idiot?"

"No, no." She shook her head. "Pretty sure he was referring to whoever he was texting with. But still, he was rude and impatient and obviously didn't want to be here." She grabbed Zach's beer and took a long swig. "I just don't understand why he came at all if he wasn't interested in having a drink."

"I'd say he's the idiot," Rex said, eyeing her. "You look hot."

Olivia side-eyed him, and with a semi-teasing voice, she asked, "Rex Holiday, are you hitting on me?"

Rex laughed. "Nope. Not at all. Just stating facts, ma'am. I've got everything I need at home."

"Good answer." She smiled appreciatively at him. "I wouldn't want to have to bust your balls. Holly deserves the best."

"Yes, she does," Rex agreed. "I'm not sure I fill that bill, but I do my best."

Zach clapped him on the shoulder. "That you do, my friend."

Olivia went on to ask Zach about Ilsa and the baby. It wasn't long before both men were knee-deep in baby stories and talking about their plans for the new year.

Chase sat back, listening to their domestic bliss, and he realized that this was what he was missing in his life. It was clearer than ever that he wanted a family. Not just any family. He wanted Lily and Evan and maybe, if she was willing, a couple more children of their own. He wanted more nights like this in the pub with his friends, laughing about life and funny things their children did.

But most of all, he wanted that connection, that love, the bond that was so clear in their relationships. All the things he'd been missing in his previous relationship. Lily's face flashed in his mind. Her sweet smile, kind eyes, and the light that lit her up from the inside. She was special. He knew that deep in his core. Was this what real love felt like? He'd loved his wife, or at least thought he had, but this seemed different. There was almost an ache in his gut when he thought about Lily and Evan. An ache that didn't seem to fade unless he was with them.

"Chase?" Zach asked.

"Yeah?" he replied, startled to realize he'd checked out of the conversation for a bit there.

"Another beer?" his friend asked.

"Nah. Thanks, though. I've got to get going. I have an early morning." He stood and tossed some cash on the table. "Thanks for the invite." Turning to Olivia, he added, "Sorry your date didn't work out. Rex is right. He's an idiot."

They all said their goodbyes and promised to get together again soon.

On the way home, Chase picked up the ingredients he needed for the Nutella cheesecake he was making and added more ingredients for homemade fudge. He'd only have time for the cheesecake that night, but he thought it would be fun to make the fudge with Evan if there was time before he left on his visit with his father.

With his hands full of groceries, Chase entered his dark house. When he flipped on the light as he walked through the living room, he heard something tumble to the floor. He glanced back and noticed that he'd flattened the photos he had on a credenza near the door.

Once he was done putting away his groceries, he doubled back and righted the frames. One was of him and his parents a few years ago when he'd been visiting Vermont. There was fresh snow on the ground and twinkle lights in their trees. It looked like an idyllic home, but he knew better. His parents loved him, but they weren't exactly close.

The other one was of him and Heather. They were at a fancy party she'd organized. Both were dressed to the nines, holding champagne glasses. He'd framed that picture because it was one of the only nights in recent memory when they'd actually had a good time. Heather had just gotten a large advertising contract to promote on her social media page and had been on cloud nine. Chase had been happy for her, and they'd spent the night celebrating.

He sat in a nearby chair, studying that picture. It hit him that it summed up his marriage to Heather. Parties, contracts, social image. All things that meant very little to him. The woman he'd married was not the woman in that picture. She'd changed, and he supposed he had too. They'd come to a fork in the road, and each had wanted a different path.

It wasn't wrong to admit that to himself. He was only just realizing that. He pressed his fingers to the glass as if touching Heather for the last time, and then instead of replacing the frame where it had been, he opened one of the credenza drawers and placed it inside. He hesitated a moment before slowly closing the drawer as if he was closing the door on his past.

It was definitely time to move on.

Feeling a sense of closure, Chase made his way into his kitchen and got to work on his cheesecake. By the time he crawled into bed, he felt a sense of accomplishment and was ready for what the next day would bring.

Chase's dream appeared in vivid colors. He was sitting in his old house at the white marble table next to the floor-to-ceiling windows that looked out over the city lights. The bright-white walls were covered in pops of colorful artwork in yellows, reds, and orange. It was very modern and beautiful but lacked the warmth he sought in his new life.

The sound of high heels clacking on the wood floors filled his ears, and he looked up to see Heather clad in a formfitting red dress with red stilettos. Her hair was styled in perfect waves that came down to her shoulders. She smiled as she sat in the chair across from him.

"Hi, Chase," she said, her eyes soft with affection.

Chase felt a tug of regret as he gazed at his beautiful wife. Her lips were painted red, and her smoky eye make-up gave her a sophistication that never failed to intrigue him. "Hello, Heather."

"It's been a long time," she said, reaching her hand out for his.

He didn't hesitate to place his hand over her open palm. "It has. A lot has changed."

"Not that much. You're still the same person you always were."

He chuckled. "So are you."

Her smile faded. "I'm sorry for... everything. I know I wasn't always easy to deal with while I was trying to build my career."

Chase sucked in a long breath. "I'm sorry, too. I wasn't always the most understanding."

They were the words they should've said a long time ago. The start of a conversation they should have had the courage to have when everything started to go south.

"I wish we could have a do-over," she said, staring at their connected hands. "I would've done a lot of things differently."

He wasn't sure that was true. "Would you have though?"

Heather gave him a wry smile. "Probably not when it comes to my career, but with us? Definitely."

Chase nodded. "I suppose that's the case with me, too. Communication always was a problem for us."

"I just want you to know that if I had the opportunity for another *chance with you, I'd take it. Through it all, I really did love you. I still do."*

"I love you, too," he said, meaning it. "But I have to move on now. You understand that, right?"

She nodded, her smile turning sad and regretful. "You're the best man I know, Chase. I just want you to have the best in life."

He squeezed her hand. "I'm working on it."

CHAPTER NINETEEN

*L*ily woke with a start. Her pulse was racing, and she felt disoriented as she blinked, trying to focus on her familiar surroundings. Her cozy room with the patchwork quilt, the steel blue wall, and the large picture window with a view of the redwoods was a far cry from the modern downtown home she'd witnessed in Chase's dream.

Lily hadn't dreamwalked anyone since the night she'd walked into Sean's dream and was tipped off that he was likely cheating on her. That dream had left her devastated. This one left her sad and a little guilty for intruding on Chase's dreams. She hadn't meant to. And although it wasn't something she could really control, sometimes she could walk out if she realized what was going on. This time she hadn't even tried. She'd been too caught up in the dark beauty of it all.

Chase had told her that things with his wife hadn't been perfect, but judging by what she'd just witnessed, he'd at least believed that they loved and respected each other. That much was clear. It made her heart ache for him. For the fact that he lost her before they could resolve their issues. And for herself.

It didn't feel great being privy to his private relationship with his late wife. To realize that he still loved her even when he'd said it was time to move on.

His wife was gorgeous. Accomplished. How was she supposed to compete with that? She blew out a breath and buried her face in her hands. This wasn't normal. She hated that her ability thrust her into the minds of people she cared about. While it had done her a favor with her ex, she didn't really want to know how Chase felt about his wife.

Those were his private thoughts, and he was entitled to them. She jumped out of bed and went straight to the shower. After setting the hot water to practically scalding, she stood under the stream and willed the water to wash away the unease that came from invading Chase's dreams.

When she emerged, her skin was splotchy and her mind determined. She only had a few more days until Evan left for the Christmas holiday with his father, and she was determined to make the best of it.

THE WORKDAY FLEW BY. Between the online orders and people stopping in for holiday treats, Lily hadn't even had a chance to do anything other than say hi to Chase. When it was quitting time, she stopped in the back room and said, "Hey there, stranger."

His lips curved into a smile as he glanced over at her. He had a smudge of chocolate on his cheek and Lily had a sudden vision of herself licking it off. Chase wiped his hands on a towel and moved toward her. "Hey yourself. Are you heading out?"

She nodded. "Just checking to see what time we can expect you tonight."

Chase glanced at the clock. "I should be done here in an hour or so. How does six sound?"

"Perfect. Dinner will be done about six-thirty."

"Do you have any plans for after dinner?" he asked. "If not, I bought supplies for fudge and was thinking Evan might like to help me make a batch."

Butterflies fluttered in her stomach, making her feel like a sixteen-year old who'd just been asked to the prom or something. What was wrong with her? The man was a chocolatier, and her son had an interest in baking. This wasn't a stretch. She ordered herself to calm down and said, "I think he'd love that. Do I need anything special? I can run by the store on the way home."

"Nothing at all. Just Evan and the stove." He winked. "See you later."

Lily waved and hurried out of there before she made good on the desire to lick his face. Or press him up against the wall and kiss the heck out of him. The man was just too good to be true. Or was he? Even after admitting that his marriage had some issues, he'd still seemed to love his wife if his dream was anything to go by.

Lily pulled into the parking lot of the Frost Family Christmas Tree Farm and hurried down the path to Ilsa's house. The door flew open to expose a room full of wrapping paper and laughter just as Lily was about to knock.

"Mom!" Evan cried and hurled himself at her, giving her a big hug.

"Hey, buddy. What did I do to deserve this reception?" she asked, bewildered. She and her son were close, but this wasn't exactly his normal greeting.

"Come in. I have something to show you." He tugged her by her hand and over to the table where Vin was busy handwriting invitations. "Zach and Ilsa are having a New Years' Eve party with a bonfire and they said Vin can have a few of his friends spend the night. Can I go? They're going to have sleigh rides and a movie marathon. Ilsa said I can bake the cookies."

Lily's heart sank as she looked over at Ilsa. Her friend was busy feeding Mia and grinning at Lily. It had been a few days since Lily had filled her in on what was happening in her life, and Ilsa would have no way of knowing that Evan was supposed to be out of town. Otherwise, Lily was sure she wouldn't have hyped the party so much. "We'll have to talk to your dad about it, Evan."

Her son's face fell, and he stared at the ground as he said, "Do you think he'll let me come home early?"

Oof. That was the look of a boy who knew this was going to be a tough battle. Still, she didn't want to crush his hope in front of everyone. She squeezed his hand. "I really don't know what he'll say, but we'll try, okay?"

He raised his eyes to her and nodded, but he already looked defeated.

Lily wanted to scream out her frustration. She knew it was just a New Year's Eve party, and the Frosts would have others that Evan would likely be invited to, but this was new for him. He hadn't been to one before in Christmas Grove, and she knew this would be a major disappointment for him.

"You mean Evan can't go to the party?" Vin asked as his brow furrowed in concern. "Why not?"

"Vin," Ilsa said mildly. "Lily and Evan might already have other plans."

"Doing what?" Vin asked.

Lily sighed. "Evan is going to be spending time with his dad over the holiday. He might not be in town."

"Oh, okay." Vin nodded solemnly. He knew all about splitting time between parents. While he lived with Ilsa and Zach full-time now, he also went back and forth with his mother, Whitney, when she wasn't busy traveling for her new job. "I get it."

Ilsa gave Lily a sympathetic smile and said, "It'll all work out."

"I hope so." Lily walked over to Ilsa and gave Mia a kiss. "Hello, pretty girl."

Mia let out a squeal of delight and kissed Lily back. Lily couldn't help laughing. She was just so darned cute with her dark curls and rosy pink cheeks.

"Okay, troublemaker," Lily said. "Evan and I have plans, so we have to get going. But we'll see you soon."

"Bye!" Mia waved her spoon and giggled.

"Goodness, those dimples," Lily said. "You're gonna be in serious trouble with this one," she teased Ilsa.

Ilsa snorted. "No kidding. Pray for me, okay?"

"Always." Lily kissed Ilsa on the cheek, and then they said their goodbyes. Once they were in Lily's car, Evan turned and stared out the window.

"Hey," Lily asked him. "How are you doing?"

He shrugged one shoulder.

"Chase is coming over tonight. He'd really like your help making fudge. How does that sound?"

Evan turned to her, and his lips curved into a hint of a smile. "Really? He wants my help?"

"Yep. He asked specifically if you could help him."

"Sure. I don't think I've ever made fudge. Have I?"

Lily shook her head. "Nope. Not with me anyway."

His smile grew, and Lily's heart felt lighter. If Sean was going to disappoint him, and Lily was sure he would, at least Evan had his time with Chase to look forward to.

By the time they walked into the house, Evan was chatting away happily about a new cookie he wanted to make.

"Maybe later," Lily said. "Right now I need to get started on dinner."

"I'll help." He led the way to the kitchen, and the pair of them got to work.

Forty minutes later, Lily was happy and relaxed when she put the lasagna in the oven. After cleaning up their mess, she was startled when she turned around and found Evan watching her from across the kitchen. "What is it? Do I have sauce all over me or something?"

"Are you going to call Dad?"

She blinked, caught totally off guard. "Um, sure."

"I want to let Vin know if I'll be able to go to the party."

"Right." Lily should've known he wouldn't forget about the New Year's Eve bash. That had been wishful thinking because she absolutely did not want to call Sean. She wanted to forget about him until he arrived on Saturday to take Evan to Tahoe. "I'll give him a call tonight and see what I can do."

He ran over and hugged her. "Thanks, Mom."

She ran her hand over the back of his head as she hugged him back. "You're welcome, kid. But remember, it's up to your dad. So we'll have to see what he says."

He nodded. "Okay."

The doorbell rang and Evan sprang into action. He ran to the front door and flung it open. "Mom! Chase is here."

Lily, who was standing behind her son, met Chase's amused gaze and laughed. "Thanks, Evan."

He spun around. "Oh. I didn't know you were there."

"Obviously." She gestured to Chase. "Come on in. Dinner's in the oven."

"It's smells wonderful," Chase said as he moved into the house with a tote bag in his hand.

"Kitchen's that way." Lily gestured behind her. "Feel free to unpack your goods."

"Thanks." He leaned in and kissed her on the cheek.

Evan grabbed one of Chase's hands and tugged him into the kitchen. He started asking rapid fire questions about how to make fudge.

Lily watched them for a few moments and was surprised at the contentment that washed over her. She liked seeing them together. Her phone beeped, startling her. A strange sense of dread formed in the pit of her stomach. Was Sean messaging her?

She fished her phone out of her pocket and sighed in relief when it was just her dad asking if he needed to pick Evan up from school the next day. She quickly texted him back with a yes and thanked him for his help.

After the text went through, Lily stared at her phone and then sank down onto her chair. It frustrated her that she was suddenly dreading the possibility of her ex contacting her. Why was she allowing him to have any sort of power over her? She'd left him for a reason. This was her life, and she would not let him intimidate her anymore.

Lily sat up, straightened her spine, and called Sean.

"We're in the middle of dinner, Lily," Sean said when he finally answered. "What is it? Is my son okay?"

"Good evening to you, too," she said, more than a little annoyed. If he was so worried about Evan's wellbeing, where had he been for the last three years? "Evan is fine. But he is why I'm calling."

The sound of chatter and restaurant din filtered over the phone. Sean said something, but his voice was muffled as if he were talking to someone else.

"Sean?"

"I'm here. Give me a minute. I can't have this conversation at the table."

Lily waited until the background noise disappeared and Sean came back on the line.

"What is this about, Lily?" he asked.

"Evan was invited to a New Year's Eve party and he really—"

Sean cut her off. "Evan will be with me and Melissa on New Year's Eve. Is this really what you called to ask me about?"

"Yes, it is. Evan asked me to call because it's important to him. He hasn't really had an opportunity to participate in something like this before, and he really wants to be there with his friend."

"This is ridiculous, Lily. He's eight. There will be other parties."

Lily clutched her phone so hard her fingers ached. "Eleven."

"What?"

"He's eleven, Sean. Your son is eleven."

"Right. Well, the answer is no. I'm not bringing him back early for some kid's party. Evan will spend the evening with me and Melissa, and that's all there is to it."

She'd expected this from him. He'd always been far too authoritarian with Evan when they'd still been together. But she'd hoped for her son's sake that he'd at least consider Evan's request. "Can you at least consider it? Wouldn't you rather spend a romantic New Year's Eve with your fiancée?"

"I'm not twenty-two, Lily. Melissa and I don't need to stay

up until midnight celebrating over candlelight. A night in with Evan will be just fine."

Lily swallowed a frustrated groan, and tried her best to appeal to Sean's softer side, if he even still had one. "Sean, can't you just take into consideration that this is important to him? He's had a rough time the past few years and has finally found his place here in Christmas Grove. This is the first party he's been invited to, and he really wants to go. I'm not asking for myself. I'm asking for him."

"You're really asking me to drive Evan over the mountain early just for a party?"

"You don't have to. I'll come get him," she offered.

"In your car?" he asked with a huff of laughter. "You aren't seriously going to drive that over the mountain, are you?"

"Sean... There is nothing wrong with my car. But if it bothers you, I'm sure I can get a friend to help out."

"You mean that guy you're dating?" His voice was full of scorn. "Is that him in the background right now?"

Lily glanced over at the kitchen where Chase and Evan had their heads together, poring over a recipe book. "Does it really matter?"

"Yes. It does. I already told you I don't approve of your *boyfriend* being around my son. The last thing I'm going to let you do is pick Evan up early so he can play father and husband to *my* family."

"Is that what all this is about?" Lily accused as she got up and started pacing her living room. "You're jealous that I'm dating someone? You're engaged to be married, Sean. We've been divorced for three years."

"I'm not jealous," he snarled. "I just don't want some stranger acting like Evan's father. I'll tell you what, Lily. If it's so important to you that Evan be able to go to this party, I'll make you a deal."

Trepidation washed over her. She just knew that whatever he said, she wasn't going to like it. "What deal?"

"You stop seeing that guy, and I'll bring Evan home early." The smugness in his tone was enough to make Lily lose it.

"Are you serious?" she hissed into the phone. "You're trying to manipulate me at the expense of our son? What is wrong with you?"

"I'm not manipulating anything, Lily. You just have a choice to make. Who will it be? Your boyfriend or your son?"

"You're a bastard," she said.

"I've heard that before. Let me know what you decide."

The call ended and Lily wanted to scream. She immediately scrolled through her contacts and was about to call her lawyer when the buzzer from the oven sounded, indicating dinner was ready.

"Son of a… ugh!" she muttered to herself.

"Lily? Do you want us to take this out of the oven?" Chase called from the kitchen.

"Yes, please," she forced out. "I'll be there in a minute." Without waiting for an answer, she rushed off to the bathroom to collect herself before she faced her son.

CHAPTER TWENTY

$\mathcal{C}$hase busied himself with buttering the garlic bread while he waited for Lily to return to the kitchen. He hadn't intended to listen in on her phone call, but he'd gotten enough from her side of the conversation to understand that her ex had been a major A-hole. He wasn't the only one either. Evan clearly heard just as much and understood that his father had been less than cooperative.

"Hey," Chase said. "Want to help me spread the garlic butter on this bread?"

"Sure." Evan stood on the other side of the island counter and got to work on the slices of bread.

"I heard you're supposed to do some baking for your school this week. Something about a fundraiser?" Chase prompted.

"Yeah." Evan kept his eyes focused on the bread as he slowly buttered a piece.

"Do you want some help? I'm generally free most evenings," Chase offered.

Evan jerked his head up. "Really?"

"Sure. I'll be your assistant. You can teach me a few things."

"My assistant?" Evan giggled. "You mean I can make you wash the mixing bowls?"

"If that's what you need." Chase wrapped the loaf of bread into tinfoil and popped it into the oven. "But I'm also pretty good at decorating, if you're making cookies that need decorations."

"Oh, yeah." Evan scooted around the island and pulled out his phone. He pulled up a website that showed cookies that looked like they'd been airbrushed. "Can you do something like this?"

"Yep. It requires some special equipment, but I can bring mine if you want," Chase said.

"Yes!" He bounced on the balls of his feet and beamed.

"Hey, you two," Lily said as she appeared in the doorway of the kitchen. "What is this I hear about airbrushed cookies?"

Evan rushed over to her and held his phone out. "Chase is going to help me make these for the holiday fundraiser."

Lily's eyebrows shot up. "You're going to make those? Wow. Fancy."

"He says he has the equipment and will be my assistant." Evan was so excited he could barely hold still.

"That's more than kind of him," Lily said, giving Chase a grateful look. She mouthed *thank you* in his direction.

"I'm just happy to have a reason to break out the airbrush," Chase told them both as Lily opened a cabinet and grabbed some plates. He took them from her and started to set the table.

The three of them sat down to dinner, and through the entire meal, Evan talked about the cookies he wanted to make and brainstormed design ideas. By the time dinner was over, Chase had written down over two dozen ideas.

"I'm not sure we'll get to all of these, but we can certainly try," Chase told him.

Lily sat back in her chair, sipping a glass of wine, her eyes bright as she watched them. She'd been quiet for most of the meal, preferring to sit back with an amused smile as she let them do their thing. The few times Chase tried to draw her into the conversation, she turned it back to Evan, letting him take the lead.

"You can do it. I know you can," Evan said, already unpacking Chase's tote and placing the fudge ingredients on the counter.

"Hey now. Let's clean up dinner first," Chase said as he turned the water on and started rinsing the plates.

"You don't have to do that," Lily said, trying to nudge him out of the way.

"What?" Chase asked, standing his ground. "No way. The cook does not clean. That's the rule."

Lily gave him a cute half smile. "Seriously?"

"Seriously," he said with a nod. "Go sit down and relax. We've got this."

"Fine," she said. "You clean up dinner, and I'll clean up after the fudge."

"Nope," Chase said, shaking his head. "We'll do that as we go." He pointed toward the table. "Relax, and one of us will bring you dessert and coffee. Regular or decaf?"

She snorted out a laugh and said, "Decaf."

"We're on it." Chase let Evan take over the dishes as he made the coffee and got out the Nutella cheesecake. Once the dishes were done, he served the cheesecake and coffee.

As expected, Evan plowed through his dessert as if he hadn't eaten in days.

Lily took her time, savoring each bite and nearly driving

Chase mad every time she wrapped her lips around the fork. "Stop staring at me like that," she whispered when Evan took his plate to the sink.

"I can't help it," Chase teased. "You keep doing that thing with your mouth."

She clamped her mouth shut, making him laugh.

"Are you done?" Evan asked Chase.

He glanced down at his own half-eaten cheesecake. "Not quite."

Evan tapped his foot.

"Evan," Lily warned. "Stop being rude. Chase will tell you when he's ready to start the fudge."

Her son let out a grunt of irritation. "Fine. Call me when you're ready." He took off into the other room, and shortly after, they heard his footsteps above them.

"What's he doing up there?" Chase asked.

Lily shrugged. "He's probably going to play a game on his computer."

Chase laughed. "Great. Now we'll never get him back down here."

"Normally I'd agree," Lily said. "But not when you're here and going to teach him how to make something he's never made before. One call from you, and he'll be right back down here."

Chase sobered. "Are you okay?"

"Yeah, why?" she asked.

"The call with your ex earlier," Chase said. "You don't have to talk about it. I just heard some of your end of the conversation, and it didn't sound like it went very well."

She closed her eyes and leaned back in her chair. "You heard that?"

"Some of it," he said and then grimaced. "Most of it, actually."

"Did Evan hear, too?" She opened her eyes, looking pained.

"Yeah. He got the gist."

"Dang it." She pressed a hand to her forehead. "I wanted to tell him about it later."

"What was it about? If you don't mind me asking," Chase asked. He'd decided earlier to not say anything about it, but he just couldn't let it go. Lily's ex seemed like such a jerk that he wanted her to feel supported if she needed someone to talk to.

"It's fine," Lily said, waving her hand. "Evan wants to go to the New Year's Eve party at Ilsa and Zach's. His dad isn't having it, even though he's been MIA for years." She sucked in a sharp breath and added, "And then when I went to bat for him, he tried to make a deal with me."

Chase frowned, not liking the sound of that at all. "What deal?"

She hesitated for a moment before she blurted, "He said Evan could go if I stopped seeing you."

"He wants you to stop seeing me?" Chase asked, dumbfounded. "Why?"

She held her hands up in an I-don't-know gesture. "My guess is it's an ego thing. He doesn't like it that we're moving on with our lives." She sat back and shook her head. "He even still thinks of Evan as an eight-year-old. It's like time has stood still for him. It's ridiculous."

Chase rubbed at a spot on his chest. It had started aching the moment she'd revealed her ex was trying to get her to stop seeing him. "What did you say?"

"I told him he's a bastard," she said.

"No argument there," Chase said, nodding. But that wasn't the answer he was looking for. "Did you give him an answer?"

"To his absurd ultimatum? No. And he hung up on me before I could tell him to go to hell."

Chase blew out a breath, relieved she wasn't letting him manipulate her. "I really hate your ex."

"That makes two of us." Lily rose, picked up her dessert plate, and called, "Evan! Chase is ready to make fudge now."

Chase glanced down at his still half-eaten cheesecake and realized Lily was more than ready to stop thinking about her ex. He knew how to take a hint, so he got to his feet, ready to teach Evan everything there was to know about making fudge.

An hour later when the fudge was in the fridge and the kitchen was clean, Evan gave Chase a big hug. "Thank you," Evan said, holding on tight.

"You're welcome. I've never had a better sous chef," Chase assured him.

Evan held on tighter, and when he let go, he ran past his mother and straight upstairs.

Lily stared after him, her mouth slightly open. Then her gaze shifted to Chase. "He's getting really attached to you."

Chase wasn't sure how he was supposed to answer that. "Is that a bad thing?"

"I don't know," she said, furrowing her brow. "It is if you're only in his life temporarily. But if you plan to stick around, then no."

"And what about your ex? Is he going to have a problem with me spending time with Evan?" Chase asked.

"He already does," Lily said. Her gaze was steady and her voice firm when she added, "But I don't care what he thinks. He left us long before we left him, and that chapter of my life is over. Sean doesn't get any say in what I do or who I do it with. If Evan and I want you in our lives, then that's up to us. Not him."

Chase's heart skipped a beat, and he could have sworn it was going to thump right out of his chest. This beautiful woman standing in front of him was likely the strongest woman he knew. But still, he wasn't naive. If her ex was making noise about Chase being in her life, it wasn't a stretch to guess that he'd escalate if he didn't get what he wanted. "You have no idea how happy I am to hear that. You're right. He doesn't get a say in your love life. That's for you to decide. But do you think he'll make things harder for you two if we keep spending time together?"

"Honestly, Chase," she said, looking tired. "Yes. I do think he'll make things harder on us, but I'm not giving one inch. I may have been a pushover in our marriage, but I'm not one now. If he wants a fight, then that's what I'll do. Thanks to you, I have a lawyer in my corner, and I'm not afraid to use her."

"Good for you, Lily," he said, squeezing her hand in support. Helping her find the lawyer was the single best thing he'd done all year. It was obvious having the lawyer on her side was giving Lily the confidence she needed to do what was right for both her and Evan.

She squeezed his hand back in response and then very quietly said, "I'd better go talk to Evan. If he heard the phone call, then I need to let him know his father hasn't made a decision."

"He hasn't?" Chase asked, wondering what that meant.

"No, he hung up on me before I could refuse to play his games. Which means I'm not done advocating on Evan's behalf."

"That's my girl." Chase tugged her to him and gave her a soft kiss. He'd do anything to lead her upstairs to her bed and spend the night holding her, but he knew she wasn't ready for him to spend the night. Instead, he kissed her one more time and said, "Goodnight, Lily. Dinner was delicious."

She wrapped her arms around him, hugging him almost as hard as her son had. "So was dessert."

He chuckled. "I think that's why we make a good team."

"Oh, that's it?" She laughed. "Well, it's a start at least."

Lily walked him to the door, and after a few more stolen kisses, Chase closed the door behind him and went home.

His place suddenly felt too big, too empty. The three-bedroom house had seemed like a good idea when he'd purchased it, but without anyone to fill those extra rooms, his home just seemed cold, void of any warmth. He glanced around at the tasteful furniture and wished for something with more character. Something more worn to show that it was used regularly by people he loved.

The loneliness hit him out of nowhere, and instead of wallowing in his silent house, he climbed the stairs and went to bed. His thoughts raced with Lily and Evan as he drifted off to sleep.

The dream overtook him almost instantly.

Warmth spread in Chase's belly as he watched the two people he loved most in the world sit in his living room, drinking mugs of hot cocoa. They were both dressed in their pajamas, and Evan was bouncing up and down, nearly coming out of his skin with excitement.

"Where's Chase?" Evan asked.

"I think he's still in bed," Lily said, smoothing his hair down.

"But it's Christmas morning," Evan said. "Isn't it illegal to sleep in?"

Lily laughed. "No. It isn't. And he was up late last night replenishing Santa's cookie tray."

They both glanced over at the tray of cookies Chase had filled the night before. *All of them were gone except for one, and it had a bite out of it.*

"Who ate the cookies?" Evan demanded.

Lily inspected the cookies and held up the last one on the tray. Someone had taken a bite and put it back. "Was this you, Evan, or the Christmas elves?"

"It wasn't me," Evan insisted, looking indignant. The expression cleared just as fast and he ran over to the tree and held a present up high in the air. "It was elves! Look, Mom. They left me something."

Lily grinned. "That's cool. But you can't open it until Chase comes down."

Evan's excitement deflated as he sank back down to the floor. "How long will that be?"

"It doesn't look like you need to wait any longer," Chase said, standing at the top of the stairs in pajama bottoms but no top.

"Merry Christmas, Chase!" Evan called and then immediately started to tear open the paper on his present.

Lily chuckled softly as she watched her son have the time of his life.

Chase moved into the room, dropped a kiss on Evan's head, and then sat next to Lily and pulled her in with a one-armed hug. "Merry Christmas, my lovely wife."

Lily kissed him and whispered, "Merry Christmas, husband."

CHAPTER TWENTY-ONE

*L*ily stared up at her ceiling, clutching at her heart. Tears fell silently down her temples as emotion overwhelmed her. She'd only been asleep for short time before she'd walked right into Chase's dreams again. The Christmas scene had been everything she'd ever wanted for herself and Evan. It had been both beautiful and painful.

Beautiful because it was a dream she shared, but painful because she was afraid to hope that she and Chase might one day have that life. That the three of them would be sharing Christmas together, and that they would be happily married.

When she'd married Sean, she'd gone into it with just as many hopes and dreams, but it hadn't taken long for every last one to be squashed into oblivion. He hadn't valued his family. He'd only valued himself and what he wanted. The hardest part was that she hadn't seen it before she'd committed herself to him. And while she knew and understood that Chase was a very different person, it also meant she just didn't trust her own judgment.

If she gave her heart fully to Chase, would he crush it, too?

Deep in her heart, she didn't think so, but how could she be sure? She had no idea. Sighing, she turned on her side and closed her eyes, willing sleep to return.

When Lily opened her eyes again, she squinted in the pale light of the predawn. Her eyes were gritty, and her body felt weighted down with exhaustion. She hadn't slept well, and she was unsettled. She'd definitely gotten too close to Chase too fast. Even if his dream had only been a dream and he wasn't ready for marriage and family, it was still too soon to even be thinking about taking that step.

She rubbed at her eyes and dragged herself to the shower.

Once she was dressed and ready for work, Lily made her way downstairs to find her son had already made them breakfast. There were pancakes on the table with toast and orange juice. She chuckled to herself. "Looks like a carb fest in here."

He spun around with a spatula in his hand and an apron tied around his waist.

"Look at you, Mr. Emeril Lagasse," she said, waving a hand at him. "I didn't realize I was going to get the personal chef treatment."

"Who's that?" he asked, frowning.

"A chef with his own television show." She sat at the table and picked up a piece of toast. It was still warm, and Evan had already buttered it to perfection. "This is great, Ev. Thank you."

He grinned, his entire face lighting up with pleasure. "You're welcome." He set a cup of coffee in front of her and said, "I'm not sure I got the coffee measurements right."

Lily eyed the dark roast in her cup. When she held it up, the aroma made her mouth water. "It smells great."

"Taste it," he said nervously.

She took a sip. It was stronger than she usually made it, but then she was known to skimp on grounds just to make it last longer. "It's wonderful, kid. Sit down and have breakfast with me."

Evan grabbed another glass of orange juice and sat next to her. "I would've made bacon or sausage to go with this, but I think we're out."

Lily nodded. It wasn't often that she purchased breakfast meats. It just wasn't in the budget. Usually she made eggs for their protein, or she added some protein powder to a smoothie.

"This is perfect," she said, even though she knew she was going to be in desperate need of a nap within a few hours. Considering her lack of sleep and the carb coma waiting for her, she'd be lucky if she wasn't yawning in customers' faces.

"Chase said it would be nice to make you breakfast every once in a while," he said to his plate.

"He did?" she asked, astonished. "Why?" Lily cleared her throat. "I mean, how did that conversation come up?"

Her son gave her a shy smile. "I was talking about how I wanted pancakes for breakfast, but you always make eggs, and that's when he told me it might be nice if I took breakfast on myself, since I obviously knew my way around the kitchen."

Lily laughed. "So this was really all because you wanted pancakes?"

He flushed. "Not only because I wanted pancakes. Chase said you work hard and that it wouldn't hurt for me to show my appreciation, so I made breakfast."

A rush of gratitude for Chase had her shaking her head in disbelief. How was this guy real? Not only had he managed to work his way into her heart, he'd obviously done the same with her son, to the point that Evan was listening to his advice. Their relationship was barreling full speed ahead, and if Lily wasn't careful, she thought they might crash hard. She needed to slow this down. It wasn't that she didn't appreciate Chase and his relationship with Evan, it was just too much too fast.

"This is very sweet of you, Evan. I do appreciate it very much." She hugged her son, and despite her reservations about her relationship with Chase, she was grateful for his presence in their lives. She just didn't know what to do next.

~

BEING that it was just a week before Christmas, the shop was as busy as usual. Chase spent the entire day working in the back, while Ilsa and Lily ran nonstop. By the end of the day, Lily was looking forward to kicking her feet up and watching Netflix with a fire in the fireplace. Her dad was taking Evan to the bakeoff, giving Lily a much-needed break.

As they were closing down, Ilsa stepped up next to her and said, "Holly and I are going to grab dinner at Mistletoe's. We'd love it if you could join us. I know Evan has that baking thing, but Zach is going to be there with Vin. He can keep an eye on things for you."

Lily glanced over at Chase, who was now standing in the doorway watching them. She quickly glanced away. "I was actually going to have a Netflix night with my feet up. My dad's taking Evan to the bakeoff."

"A night alone with Netflix sounds divine," Ilsa said with a sigh. But then she lowered her voice and added, "But won't you have plenty of time for that next week while Evan is out of town?"

A small ache formed in Lily's gut as she nodded. "Yeah. I just didn't have it in me to do the bakeoff."

"Come to dinner with us," Ilsa urged. "It won't be a long

night. Just long enough to get caught up and have someone else feed us for a change."

"Yeah, okay," she said. It wasn't often she got to spend time with her friends without kids or their husbands. "I'll be there."

Ilsa grinned. "Great. See you at six at Mistletoe's."

"I'll be there."

Her friend nodded and disappeared into the back to work on some end-of-day paperwork.

Chase moved to stand next to her. "Hey. I haven't had a chance to talk to you all day."

"Yeah, it's been busy." Lily continued to clean the counters, putting items away for the day.

"Is everything all right?" he asked.

"Sure."

Chase frowned. "You seem... distracted."

She stopped what she was doing and turned to face him. "Listen, Chase. I'm just tired and a little overwhelmed by everything."

"By everything, do you mean me?" he asked.

Lily held back a grimace. She guessed there was something to be said for a man who knew how to communicate. "You. My ex. The fact that Evan is getting very attached to you. He made me breakfast this morning, by the way. I learned I have you to thank for that."

His eyebrows shot up. "Should I be apologizing for that?"

Son of a... She squeezed her eyes shut, hating that she sounded so ungrateful. "No." She stared up at him. "It's just that you and Evan are getting very close. And you're a great guy, so that's not a bad thing. It just scares me. I need time to process."

He blinked. "Do you want me to step away from the bakeoff tonight?"

"No," she said again. "Evan would be very disappointed. I just..." She threw her hands up. "Do you understand my hesitation at all? This is moving fast, and Evan will be devastated if things don't work out. I'm not even sure what I'm asking for. All I know is that I need to process this before we spend more time together."

"Okay," he said. "I get it. But I think you should know I'd still be Evan's friend even if you decide we're not the right fit romantically. I like him. We have a lot in common."

"Yeah? Besides baking, what else?" she asked, curious as to what he'd say.

"Trains for one. And we both like you." He gave her a kind smile and then cupped her cheek briefly. "I don't want to pressure you, Lily. I just want you to know that I really like both of you. And when you're ready, I'll be here." He leaned in, kissed her on the cheek, and then left her alone to finish her end-of-day tasks.

"TELL US EVERYTHING," Ilsa demanded the moment Lily took her seat at Mistletoe's.

Lily let out an exaggerated sigh. "Can I get a drink first?"

The waitress seemed to magically appear with water and asked what else she could bring them. Lily ordered a glass of wine while the other two went with fancy cocktails that would likely put Lily under the table. She didn't drink often, and her tolerance was almost nonexistent.

"Okay, drinks ordered," Holly said. "What is going on with you and Chase?"

Both of Lily's friends were leaning forward, nearly bouncing in their seats for the gossip.

Lily sat back in her seat and crossed her arms over her chest.

"Uh oh. That doesn't look good," Ilsa said, frowning.

"Not good at all," Holly agreed. "What happened?"

"Nothing happened," Lily said, frustrated at herself more than anything. "He's great. Better than great. He's a freakin' saint. The man is considerate, he gets along with my kid, cooks, bakes, has a stable job, is kind to everyone, and treats me better than anyone ever has before."

Holly and Ilsa shared a knowing look.

"What?" Lily demanded.

"You're scared," Ilsa said gently and placed her hand over Lily's. "We've both been there before."

"Yeah, well. My kid loves him. If this doesn't work out, he's going to be devastated," Lily said.

Holly gave her a sympathetic smile. "Evan's not the only one who's going to be devastated."

"You're not wrong," Lily admitted. "But I'll be okay. I just don't want to put Evan through that again. His dad already..." She waved a hand in the air. "I don't want to talk about Sean other than to say he hasn't been there for Evan."

"It's tough being a single mom and navigating dating," Ilsa said. "Neither Holly nor I have had your exact experience, but we do know what it's like to take a chance on giving our hearts to someone."

"How did you do it?" Lily asked, sounding a little desperate even to her own ears.

"A leap of faith. Plenty of courage. And the realization that it's already too late," Holly said gently. "At one point, I had to face the fact that Rex already had my heart. And it was either trust him with it, or give up the chance of happiness with the love of my life. I don't want to sound cliché, but I do think it's true when they say, 'it's better to have loved and lost than never to have loved at all.'"

Lily groaned while Ilsa chuckled. Lily eyed Ilsa. "Do you think that's true?"

Ilsa nodded. "There's no doubt that I'd be a broken devastated mess if I were to ever lose Zach, but the love he's brought to me and Mia, even if it was for a short time, is worth every bit of heartache. The question you have to ask yourself is whether Chase is that person for you."

Yes.

The answer was right there, screaming in her head. There was no doubt that Lily could fall head over heels for Chase... if she hadn't already.

Holly reached out and took Lily's other hand. "Lil, it's obvious to us what the answer to that question is. All you have to do now is find a way to be brave. I promise; it's worth it."

The drinks arrive at that moment. Lily grabbed her wine glass, nodded her acknowledgment and then drained the entire thing.

CHAPTER TWENTY-TWO

*C*hase needed to talk to Lily. He'd understood her need for a little space. Their relationship had been moving at top speed. Every time she'd indicated that she wanted to take things slow, they'd somehow sped up instead. That hadn't been his intention. It had just happened.

After the bakeoff, Chase was careful to honor her request. Evan hadn't been a fan. He'd already asked Chase if he could come over and help him learn to make new things such as crème brûlée and tiramisu. Both of those were ambitious projects, and Chase wasn't even sure where he'd come up with the idea for those particular desserts. They weren't exactly what he'd guess an eleven-year-old would want to eat, but Evan wasn't just any kid. He appreciated the hard work it took to make something great. Instead of declining, Chase had asked for a raincheck.

Even though he didn't want to push Lily, Chase had a choice to make. He'd gotten both Evan and Lily Christmas presents, and he wanted to give Evan his before he left for the holiday. When Lily was on her break at work, he joined her at her table.

"Hey," she said, sounding surprised. "What's up?"

"I know you said you wanted some time to let things settle a bit, and I'm completely cool with that. I don't want to rush you or anything, but I was wondering if I could stop by tonight. I have something for Evan for Christmas and was hoping I could give it to him before he leaves."

Warmth lit Lily's eyes, and she smiled softly at him. "I think that would be wonderful. Thank you."

Chase didn't say anything for a moment. He hadn't expected her to agree that quickly. "Are you sure?"

Lily chuckled. "Did you want me to say no?"

"No. Not at all." He placed his hands palms down on the table. "I guess I expected a little more pushback."

She nodded. "Yeah, maybe I would have if Evan wasn't leaving tomorrow. But he's been asking about you, and I don't want to disappoint him."

Chase was the one feeling disappointed. Even though she'd said it was fine for him to come over, she'd said it was so that Chase could connect with Evan. She hadn't made any mention or behaved in any way that implied she wanted to see him. And that stung a little. "Okay. I'll be by tonight then. Six okay?"

"Perfect."

He stood. "Time to get back to work."

Lily nodded, but her smile slipped as a touch of sadness shone in her eyes.

The urge to ask her what was wrong was right on the tip of his tongue, but he held it back. Now wasn't the time, and he wasn't even sure he wanted to know. "Tonight then."

"Tonight," she agreed.

NERVES MADE Chase hesitate outside Lily's door. He couldn't remember the last time he'd been nervous to spend time with a woman. But that night, he just didn't know what to expect. Was Lily going to keep that wall between them she'd erected earlier in the week? Or was this going to be like the other evenings they'd spent together? He suspected the former, but hoped it was the latter.

The door flung open before Chase even knocked, revealing Evan on the other side of the door. "Chase! What are you doing out here?"

"Hauling Christmas presents. What else?" he said cheerfully as he held up the canvas bag he'd packed with their gifts.

"Mom!" Evan called. "Santa's here."

Chase chuckled as Evan tugged him inside.

"Put them under the tree," Evan ordered. "Then hurry up and get in the kitchen. Dinner's ready."

After dropping off the gifts, Chase let Evan tug him into the kitchen. Lily was already seated at the festive table. She'd put red pillar candles in the middle and spruced them up with pine tree clippings around the bases. The plates had snowmen on them, and the wine glasses were cut crystal. He picked one up, letting the light sparkle off the facets. "These are nice."

"They were my mother's. My father gave them to me a few years ago," she said, sounding melancholy. "My grandmother gave them to her, and when I was growing up, we always used them for special occasions."

The nerves that had been plaguing Chase earlier fled. Not only did it appear that Lily's walls were down, but she'd gone to some trouble to make their evening a special celebration. "We should toast," Chase said.

"With what?" Lily asked, chuckling. "It's not like I stock champagne."

"With whatever everyone is drinking," Chase said. "Water? Soda? Wine?"

"Wine is disgusting," Evan said, wrinkling his nose.

"Speak for yourself, kid," Chase shot back with a chuckle.

Lily got up and retrieved a bottle of wine and a root beer from the fridge. After filling Evan's glass with root beer and the other two with the wine, she held her glass up. "What are we toasting?"

Chase held his glass up and nudged Evan to do the same. "How about to new friends and a safe and happy holiday?"

Lily echoed his words while Evan beamed at Chase and just said, "To new friends."

They all sipped their drinks.

Chase met and held Lily's gaze. "Thank you for tonight. I can already tell it's going to be a fantastic holiday celebration."

"You're welcome." She squeezed his arm and then lifted the lid off the platter in the middle of the table.

"Is that goat cheese-stuffed chicken?" Chase asked, his mouth already watering.

"Yep!" Evan stabbed one with the serving fork and put it on his plate.

"It's Holly's recipe," Lily said. "She gave it to me last week, and when I knew you were coming, I figured tonight was a good night to try it out. Let me know what you think."

Chase could tell just by looking at it that it would be delicious. The chicken wasn't overcooked, and the goat cheese was full of herbs. And when he took his first bite, his eyes rolled to the back of his head. Without thinking, he said, "I do love a woman who knows her way around the kitchen."

Lily choked, making her eyes water until she got control of herself again. "What did you say?"

"I just meant that I appreciate someone who knows how to cook," he said. "You know, since it aligns with my interests."

"Right." Lily rubbed her throat. "Just as long as you aren't looking for someone to cook all your meals."

"Never," he said seriously, guessing that this was a hot button issue for her. "I like to cook. And I really appreciate delicious food." He held up his fork with a piece of chicken on the end. "This, Lily Paddington, is amazing. It was a compliment."

"Yeah, Mom. This is the best chicken I've ever had."

Lily smiled at her son. "I'm glad you like it." Then she turned to Chase. "I'm glad you like it, too."

Chase nodded and went back to his chicken, determined not to stick his foot in his mouth again.

After they were done, Evan lifted the lid off another tray and said, "I have some cookies from the bakeoff for dessert."

"They're really beautiful, Chase," Lily said. "I can't believe you made those faces on the snowmen, and the detail on the Christmas trees... incredible."

Chase's cheeks heated with the praise. "I've had a lot of practice."

"Well, if Mrs. Pottson saw these, I think she'd most definitely want to stock some at Love Potions," Lily said. "I imagine they'd fly out of the store."

"They aren't chocolate though," Chase said. "I suppose I could make them out of fudge cookies or something."

"I bet she'd want them any way you made them," Lily said as she grabbed two and stood. "Now let's go into the living room. I hear Santa has arrived."

Evan took off running, while Chase shook his head and laughed.

"It's never dull around here," Lily said with a wink.

"I can see that."

"Come on." Lily slipped her hand into his and nodded toward the living room. "Ready?"

He glanced down at their joined hands and then back at her with a questioning glance.

She gave him a tiny shrug. "I guess I've had enough space."

His heart soared, and he squeezed her hand. "You have no idea how glad I am to hear that." Then he leaned over and gave her a soft kiss.

Lily smiled and whispered, "I don't think Evan's going to be patient much longer. Not when there are presents to unwrap."

He nodded and let her lead him into the living room. To his surprise, she didn't drop his hand. In fact, when they sat on the couch together, Lily clasped her other hand over their connection and told Evan to pass out the gifts.

Chase was surprised when Evan handed him two boxes. He knew money was tight for them, and the only thing he'd wanted was to spend time with them. "You guys really didn't need to get me anything."

"It's nothing fancy, so don't get too excited," Lily said, nudging his shoulder.

"I don't need fancy. Never did." He placed the boxes beside him and said, "You two should open yours first."

Evan held up the package from Chase and asked his mom, "Can I?"

She nodded.

A few seconds later, wrapping paper was strewn all over the floor and Evan was sitting on his heels, his eyes wide with wonder and shock. "You got me a train set? An *entire* set?"

Lily let out a small gasp when she saw it and also turned to him with wide eyes. "Chase, that's… too much. You shouldn't have."

"It's not too much," he said quietly. "I always wanted a set like that of my own when I was a kid, so when I saw it at Mr. Fredrick's, I knew it was what I wanted to get Evan."

"But—"

"I love it!" Evan threw himself at Chase and gave him a big hug.

Chase hugged him back. "I'm glad, Evan."

When Evan pulled away, he asked, "Will you help me put it together?"

"Sure. Whenever is good for you."

"Tonight?"

They both looked at Lily. She threw her hands up and laughed. "Sure." She set her gaze on Evan. "But not until after the rest of the gifts are opened, and you can't stay up too late. You have to get ready for your trip in the morning."

"Okay." Evan sat back down, clutching his train set as he waited for Lily and Chase to open their gifts.

Chase nodded to Lily's package. "Go on. It's your turn."

"I'm almost afraid to find out what it is after that." She nodded toward Evan.

"I hate to say it, but it's not as cool as a train set. Hopefully you'll like it anyway," Chase said, feeling nervous. He really wanted her to like her gift.

"Not a train set?" She shook her head. "How disappointing," she teased.

"You can play with mine," Evan offered.

"Thanks, kid." Lily smiled at him and then opened her gift. It took her a moment to figure out what was in the box, but when she did, Chase saw her eyes glisten with unshed tears. "You got me an e-reader?" she asked, holding it up.

"That's what it says on the box," Chase confirmed. "I hope you didn't already have one. If you do then I can exchange—"

"I don't," she said, wiping at her eyes. "There will be no exchanging." She reached over, wrapped her arms around his neck, and then right there in front of Evan, she kissed him.

Chase was frozen, unsure of what to do, but after a moment, he leaned into her and kissed her back. It was over as fast as it started, but Chase felt his heart swell. He knew that kissing him in front of her son was a big step, and he couldn't help the grin that claimed his lips. "I guess you like it then?"

"Very much." She sat back in the couch and started to tear into the box.

"Wait. There's a card in with your gift, too," Chase said.

"Really?" Lily fished around until she found the card and then pulled it out of the envelope. As soon as she opened it, a gift card fell out.

"It's to buy some books to put on your e-reader," he explained.

Lily stared at it and then at Chase. "You shouldn't have."

"Maybe, but I wanted to." He leaned over and kissed her cheek. "I know how often you two go to the library. I figured this would be a nice compliment to your habit."

"I just... This is very thoughtful, Chase." She wiped at her eyes again. "Thank you."

"You're very welcome."

"Now you!" Evan demanded, pointing at the boxes sitting next to him.

"Okay." Chase took his time just to mess with Evan.

By the time he finally pulled the paper off the box, Evan was nearly hyperventilating. "Come on, Chase! Hurry up."

"Let him open his gifts at his own pace," Lily said through her chuckles.

"Christmas only comes once a year," Chase said. "I like to savor it." But when Evan started nearly bouncing out of his chair, Chase pulled the top off the box and found a thick recipe book titled *Dessert, the French Way*. He pulled it out and started flipping through it, and he wasn't surprised when he spotted a couple of different ways to make both crème brûlée and tiramisu. He glanced up at Evan. "Did you pick this out?"

He nodded enthusiastically.

"I love it, Evan. It's just what I wanted." Chase held his arms out for the kid and Evan ran over to give him a hug. "If it's okay with your mom, when you get back from your trip, we'll pick some recipes to try. What do you say?"

"Yes!" Then he turned to his mom. "That's okay, right?"

Lily nodded. "Of course it is. Just save some for me." She gestured to the other box. "One more."

Chase opened it and found a red apron that had a lips pattern printed on it and the words *kiss the cook* scrawled across the bib. "Is this from you?" he asked Lily.

"I thought it was cute," she said shyly.

"*You're* cute. Come here." He reached for her, and this time when they kissed it was a real one. The kind that said they were together and there was no denying it now.

"Ewww, can you guys stop," Evan complained. "I still have gifts to open."

Chase pulled away from Lily and they both turned their attention to him while he opened a few more gifts from Lily. There was a gift certificate for a video game and some new clothes, but the only thing he was really interested in at the moment was the train set Chase had gotten him. After thanking his mom, he pushed his gifts aside and tore into the train set box.

Chase spent the next few hours helping Evan put it together while Lily sat on the couch reading something on her new e-reader.

Finally, when they were done and the train was circling the track they'd put up around the tree, Lily looked at the clock. "It's time to call it a night, Ev."

"Oh, Mom. Do I have to?"

"Afraid so. It's already later than normal. Say goodnight to Chase and go get ready for bed."

Evan got to his feet and walked over to Chase, giving him one more hug. "Goodnight."

Chase held him tightly and whispered, "Merry Christmas, Evan. Have a good time with your dad."

Evan looked up at him, his eyes full of emotion. "I wish I was staying here with you."

Chase's heart cracked in two right in that moment. What was he supposed to say to that? He couldn't tell him he wished the same thing. It wasn't fair to anyone, even if it was true. "You'll be back soon, and it'll be like you never left."

Evan nodded, released him, gave his mom a hug, and slowly made his way upstairs.

Chase stared at Lily with his hand over his heart. "I think he broke me."

Lily gave him a sad smile. "He loves you."

"I..." Chase swallowed. "I love him, too."

CHAPTER TWENTY-THREE

Saturday morning came too soon. Lily stood at the door, watching as Sean and his fiancée climbed out of his SUV. Melissa was just as lovely as she was the day Lily had met her at Love Potions. She was wearing all white and had a red scarf around her neck. Her blond hair was piled high on her head with a red poinsettia flower pinned to the bun.

Lily wondered what it was like to be a woman like her. While Lily had tried her best to be stylish and keep her hair and nails done while she was with Sean, she'd never reached that level of perfection. Melissa spotted her and waved excitedly before reaching back into the SUV for a package. The woman teetered on heels as she made her way up Lily's walk while Sean held back, talking on the phone.

"Good morning," Lily said as Melissa climbed the stairs to her front porch.

"Merry Christmas!" Melissa said and handed her the package.

Lily glanced at it and forced a smile. "Thank you. This really wasn't necessary."

"It's not much. Just some perfume from my new line. I always figure, what woman doesn't like a new perfume?"

This one, Lily thought but kept it to herself. Most scents that weren't natural like citrus or vanilla gave her a headache. "It's still kind of you," Lily offered. "Did you want to come in for coffee?"

Melissa glanced back at Sean, who was now pacing. "I don't think so. Sean's in a hurry to get back. I think he said something about a business meeting. We just need to get Evan, and we'll be on our way."

"I need to talk to Sean before you guys go," Lily said.

The other woman bit down on her bottom lip as she glanced back one more time. "Yeah. Okay. I'll get him."

Lily felt rather than heard her son behind her. "Are you ready, kiddo?"

"I guess." He tossed his bag on the porch and waited by his mother's side.

She held her hand out to him, wanting to hang on and never let go. But her lawyer had already warned her that if she didn't let Sean take him for the holiday, it could hurt her if they ended up in a battle for custody. She needed to be seen as reasonable and not like she was keeping Evan from his father. As much as she wanted to tell her ex to shove it, that Evan was staying home, she couldn't. But she could make sure they were all on the same page.

It was a few minutes before Melissa returned with Sean in tow.

"Good morning, Sean," Lily said, trying to keep everything friendly.

He frowned at her and shifted as if he were trying to look into her house.

Lily glanced over her shoulder. "What is it? Did you see something?"

"No. What do you want, Lily? Like Melissa told you, we're under a tight schedule." His tone was dismissive, making Lily long to deck him.

"I'd like the address of your new home and the phone number if you have a landline in case bad weather knocks out the cell towers," Lily said in as straightforward a voice as she could muster.

Sean rolled his eyes. "Is that all?" He turned to Melissa. "Can you give her what she needs?"

"Sure." Melissa dug around in her purse until she came up with a business card. She took a moment to scribble down the information and then handed it to Lily. "Feel free to call me anytime about Evan. I just can't wait to get to know him better."

Lily placed the card in her pocket and nodded. It wasn't as if she was going to be best friends with this woman. She just wanted to be sure she could get in touch with them while Evan was in their care. "Thanks."

"Ready to go, bud?" Sean asked Evan.

"Dad, can I go to Vin's New Year's Eve party? They're going to have—"

"We've already been over this," Sean said impatiently as he cut Evan off. "We're going to be in Tahoe. There will be other parties you can go to. These next couple of weeks are family time."

"But Mom's going to be here by herself," Evan said, folding his arms over his chest.

Lily hated that her son was guarded and closed off to his father. But Sean had no one to blame but himself. He should realize that he couldn't just disappear out of his kid's life and then have everything come up roses when he decided to walk back in again. "I'll be all right, Evan," she said, squeezing his hand. "I'll probably spend the day over at Ilsa's."

Evan wrapped his arms around her, clinging to her as he whispered, "I don't want to go."

Lily's heart shattered. She pulled away just enough to look him in the eye. "It's just for a couple of weeks. Everything is going to be just fine. I'll talk to you every night, and I'm sure your dad has some fun things planned. It's going to be okay. I promise."

Melissa cleared her throat. "I'm going to make our New Year's really special, Evan," she said. "You'll see. It's going to be a lot of fun. Lake Tahoe is a really special place to spend the holidays."

Lily clamped her mouth shut. It wasn't nearly as special as spending it in Christmas Grove. Or spending New Year's Eve with his best friend.

"I think calling every night is unnecessary," Sean said with a huff. "Evan isn't a baby."

Lily turned to him, and her eyes narrowed. "I'm well aware of how old my son is. I'm also aware that it's been a long time since the two of you have spent any time together. For my own peace of mind, I want to talk to Evan every night to make sure he's doing okay with the adjustment."

"I'm his father, Lily. You don't have anything to worry about," Sean snapped.

Fuming that he was arguing about this just minutes after they'd agreed, she opened her mouth to dress him down, but Melissa beat her to it.

"Sean, honey," Melissa said, placing a soft hand on his arm. "Lily's his mother. I can only imagine what it would be like to be without my child during Christmas. I don't see the harm in her calling each night to talk to him for a few minutes."

Her ex visibly softened as he nodded at his fiancée. His shoulders relaxed, and the lines around his mouth smoothed out as the tension dissipated. Her effect on him was both fascinating and deeply annoying. He hadn't ever listened to Lily like that. Not that she could remember anyway. But she supposed it was good that he appeared to genuinely love Melissa and that she could be a calming force in his life.

"Do you promise to call every night?" Evan asked Lily.

SHE NODDED. "Absolutely. And then you can tell me all about your adventures. I hear there's going to be skiing and sledding and other outdoor stuff like that."

Evan didn't look impressed. Lily wasn't surprised. He usually preferred to spend his time indoors, baking, reading, or playing video games. He liked snow and building snowmen, but skiing and athletic stuff wasn't in his wheelhouse yet. She hoped his father would find a way to make it fun for him. But knowing Sean, she had her doubts.

"Melissa, take Evan to the car. I need to talk to Lily for a moment," Sean said.

Evan stiffened.

"It's okay," Lily whispered to him. "I'll talk to you tonight."

Evan hugged her one last time and reluctantly went with Melissa to the SUV.

Once they were out of earshot, Sean turned on her. "Your lawyer sure is a piece of work. Why are you doing this right now, right before Christmas?"

"Doing what? Asking for a concrete visitation schedule?" Lily asked him.

"That, and she's talking about child support. You know I just bought a house. It's not like I have money lying around," he spat out.

Lily wanted to laugh in his face. This man with his second home, fancy SUV, and fashion-model wife had no idea what it was like to be worried about money. Instead, she kept her cool and said, "My lawyer is just looking out for my best interests, as I'm sure is the same with yours."

"Call her off, Lily, or you're going to have one hell of a custody battle on your hands come January." He gestured to the SUV. "Do you think any judge is really going to side with a single mom with three jobs instead of me and my beautiful wife, who will gladly stay home to take care of him?"

There was so much she wanted to shoot back at him. But Lily wasn't up for a fight. "I won't call her off. All I want is a concrete visitation schedule so that I'm not getting last-minute calls that disrupt our plans."

"And money. Don't forget the money. That's what it's always been about for you, hasn't it, Lily? I bet that's why you're dating that trust-fund guy. So you can find someone to take care of you again."

Lily glared at him. "You have no idea what you're talking about, Sean. Go away now. You have Evan. You got what you wanted. Now leave me alone. Let the lawyers deal with this so we're not fighting in front of our son."

"You can bet the lawyers will be dealing with this," he spat out. "I hope you're ready."

She pressed her lips together in a thin line and watched as he stalked off. Once the SUV disappeared down the road, she pulled out her phone and called the lawyer to report his threats.

CHAPTER TWENTY-FOUR

*C*hase lay on his back, gritting his teeth as he strained to tighten a nut. The wrench slipped for what seemed like the hundredth time, and he swore as he threw the wrench down. He scooted out from underneath his sink and sat up, frustrated to his core. This was not how he'd planned to spend his Sunday.

If the plumbing under his sink hadn't sprung a leak, he'd be at lunch with Lily right that moment. Instead, he was cursing at his plumbing and wondering if he had enough painkillers to ease the backache he was sure to have later.

He'd asked Lily for a raincheck, though he wasn't sure they'd have another day off together before Christmas. It wasn't the end of the world, but he'd been looking forward to experiencing the holiday lights of Christmas Grove with her.

Chase glanced at the pipe he was trying to replace and groaned. There was no time like the present to get the job done.

Two hours later with scraped knuckles and a bruised elbow, the plumbing under his sink no longer leaked. Chase dragged himself to the shower and stayed under the hot water until his fingers wrinkled.

Once he was dressed, he sat down and called his girl.

"Hey!" she said. "Did you get it fixed?"

"I think so. What are you up to right now?" he asked.

"I'm doing inventory for Zach. Why?"

He sighed. "Damn. I forgot you were working there this afternoon. I was going to ask if you wanted to go for a late lunch."

"I would've loved that, but when you canceled, I called Zach to see if they needed help. Being that it's this close to Christmas, he said he could use all the help he could get. And since I could use the money… you know."

"It's a match made in heaven," he joked. "How long will you be there? Any chance of meeting up later?"

"Sure. How about I just come over when I'm done?" she asked.

"Perfect. I'll make something sinful for dinner."

"Sinful, huh? I can't wait." There was a lightness in her tone that hadn't been there the day before. He took that to mean she was feeling a little more settled about Evan's absence.

"I'll be waiting," he said.

Lily lowered her voice and said, "Now *that* sounds sinful."

"Lily Paddington, are you flirting with me?"

"You bet. See you tonight."

Chase ended the call with a smile on his face, and his mood lifted. But then he glanced around his bachelor pad and grimaced. If he was having company, it was time to clean the place up.

～

CHASE HAD JUST GOTTEN DONE with his second shower of the day when his doorbell rang. A smile tugged at his lips. Lily was early. It just meant that they could make dinner together or skip it and have a bedroom picnic with take out. He was still fantasizing about the bedroom picnic when he pulled his door open and then froze, his mouth hanging open.

Heather.

"Hey there stranger," the tall blonde with sparkling blue eyes said. "Bet you weren't expecting me."

As soon as he heard the inflection in her voice, his brain kicked in and he realized he wasn't staring at his late wife. No, the woman on his front step was her twin sister, Hilary, who lived in New York City. Or at least the last time they'd been in touch, that's where she'd lived.

"Hilary. What are you doing here?" he asked.

"Is that anyway to greet your favorite person?" Without waiting for an answer, she threw her arms around him and planted a kiss right on his lips.

It took him a moment for his brain to catch up, but when it did, he placed his hands on her hips and moved her away from him. "What are you doing?" he asked, taking two steps back into his house.

Hilary followed him and slammed the door behind her. She let out a long breath and leaned against the door. "Sorry. That was—"

"Crazy?" he asked, wiping his mouth with the back of his hand.

"Necessary," she corrected.

Chase scoffed. "No, not necessary. And if you do that again, I'm going to have you removed from the premises. You're Heather's sister. And I have a girlfriend. What the hell were you thinking?"

She covered her face with her hands and groaned. "Can we sit?"

Irritated beyond belief, Chase led the way to his kitchen table and held out a chair for her. "Sit."

She did as she was told, and he sat across from her.

"I don't know where to start," she said.

"How about at the beginning? What made you get on a plane and come to California?" he asked.

"Do you have any coffee?" Her expression was pleading when she added, "I had to get up at two in the morning to catch my flight."

Gritting his teeth, Chase got up and made a pot of coffee. Once he filled two mugs, he returned to the table.

"Sugar?" she asked.

Without answering, he got up, grabbed the sugar and half and half from the fridge, and handed her a spoon. "Anything else?"

Hilary shook her head. "I'm good."

He took his seat and had to forcibly stop himself from drumming his fingers on the table.

She took her time doctoring her coffee and then tasting it. He recognized her stall tactic for what it was. Hilary didn't want to talk about why she'd come, but he'd just wait her out. He wasn't going anywhere.

The clock on the wall ticked loudly in the silence.

Finally, Hilary slammed her hand down on the table and said, "Fine! I'll tell you." She unbuttoned the top button of her fitted blouse as if it were choking her. Except that would've been impossible since she was already showing some cleavage.

He ignored the lace that was showing and pretended nothing had happened.

"Remember that night last year when you came out to New York to visit me?" she asked.

He nodded. Chase had taken the last of Heather's things to her sister. Pictures, a few pieces of family jewelry, some letters, all personal things he knew Hilary would want. But instead of stuffing it in a box and mailing it to her, he'd delivered it personally.

"I wanted to kiss you then," she blurted.

Chase raised both eyebrows, completely taken aback. "What? Why?"

"You were just so... wonderful to me. No one has ever been that kind, and the way you took care of me when I broke down, I just... I don't know why my sister didn't appreciate you more. You're like the perfect man," she said with a sigh and then clasped her hand over her mouth as if she couldn't believe she'd just said that out loud.

"I'm far from perfect, Hilary," he said quietly.

"Crap." She covered her face with her hands again. "I'm so embarrassed."

He would be too if he'd hit on his sibling's partner. "Hilary, why don't you tell me why you're really here? Because I'm fairly certain you knew nothing was going to happen between the two of us."

She got up and started muttering to herself and pacing.

Chase sat back, watching her, noting how different she was from her sister. Not different physically. They were identical. The only way to tell them apart was through their actions and mannerisms. While Heather had been careful, deliberate, and intentional in everything that she did, Hilary led with her heart. She was impulsive, emotional, and passionate. Under normal circumstances, he typically enjoyed spending time with

Hilary, but he preferred her in small doses and not when she surprised him by showing up on his doorstep.

Finally, she stopped and turned to him. "I'm pregnant."

"Okay," he said, not really that surprised by her news. He figured something major had happened to make her show up unannounced. "Where's the father?"

She waved her hands in the air. "Out finding himself."

Chase couldn't hold back his snort of amusement. It was just like her to hook up with someone who would need to run off and 'find himself.'

"Don't laugh. He was really sweet to me. He just doesn't have the ability to be responsible."

"That's a tough spot to be in when you're pregnant," he said, giving her a sympathetic smile.

"Exactly," she said with an emphatic nod. "And that's why when I freaked out about how I'm going to do this, I was thinking about how you always wanted kids, and that if you were the father, you'd be there through everything, no questions asked. I don't know anyone who is more responsible than you."

"So you came here to… what? Make me the responsible dad to your baby?" he asked.

"No." She grimaced. "Yes? I don't know. I guess I just got scared, and you're really the only person in my life that I trust."

Chase chuckled.

"It's not funny," she said as she flopped down on his couch.

He moved into the living room and sat in the chair across from her. "Listen, you know I'm here for you. But don't try to kiss me again. We're not ever going to be a thing. I think you know that, right?"

She nodded.

"We're already family. We'll always be family." He reached

out and squeezed her hand. "Everything is going to be okay. I promise."

Hilary pressed a hand to her stomach and stared at him with scared eyes. "I can't do this by myself."

"I know. Don't worry. We'll work it out."

She sat up and tentatively asked, "Do you think I can have a hug now?"

"As long as you keep your lips to yourself," he teased.

"Fine. But it's your loss," she teased back and then giggled.

Chase stood and opened his arms. "Come here."

Hilary pressed her head into his chest and wrapped her arms around him. They stood there like that for a long moment before she pulled back and said, "It never would've worked between us anyway. You're far too mature for me."

He laughed. "It's all right. I'm sure there's a hippy around here somewhere who is dying to be your pseudo baby daddy."

"Gods, I hope so," she said with a sigh and hugged him again.

CHAPTER TWENTY-FIVE

*L*ily sat in her car clutching the takeout bag from Mistletoe's and felt her stomach drop to her toes. She was parked across the street from Chase's house when the tall blonde strode up to the front door. The tall blonde that looked exactly like the one in Chase's dreams.

Heather. Chase's supposedly dead wife.

His door opened, and the woman flung herself at Chase. They hugged. But then she kissed him, and the next thing Lily knew, Chase pulled her into the house and the door slammed behind them.

Lily's entire body went numb with shock. She couldn't believe what she'd seen. Chase and his wife, who was very much alive. They'd kissed, just like Holly had seen in her vision. And now they were locked away in his house doing… She shook her head. She didn't want to think about what they might be doing. If she did, she'd lose it completely.

Instead, Lily put her car in gear and drove home on autopilot. Once she was inside her house, she sat at her table with a bottle of wine and wondered what the hell she'd been thinking. She'd let herself fall for someone she barely knew. Her kid had fallen for him, too.

And he was nothing more than a cheater. Just like Sean.

Lily poured herself a very large glass of wine and sat at her table, cursing men while drowning herself in chardonnay.

She wasn't sure how long she sat there, but eventually her phone rang and Chase's name flashed on the screen. She glared at it and screamed, "Cheater! All men suck. But you suck worse because you lied about your wife dying!" She threw the phone and barely noticed when it crashed against the wall.

She took her wine bottle and moved to her living room, where she sat in the dark and contemplated what her life would be like after Evan grew up and moved out. Maybe she'd travel. Or open her own business. She had no idea what kind of business, but if she wasn't going to have a personal life and no one to care for, she could take some risks.

Or she could just get cats. Definitely cats.

The phone rang again. She ignored it. But then she wondered if it was Evan and ran back to the kitchen to find that the screen had cracked. But she could still make out the word *Dad* as the incoming caller. She answered, "Dad?"

"Hey, honey. I was just calling to see how you're doing."

"Fine. If you call being humili… humili… what's the word again?"

"Humiliated?" he asked.

"Yeah. That one." She flopped on the floor and hit her elbow on the wall, but she barely felt it.

"Lily, what's going on?" her father asked.

"I have absolutely no idea." She let out a hiccup that sounded a lot more like a sob.

"I'm coming over," her dad said.

"Fine." Lily ended the call and sat against the wall on the floor as tears started to fall unchecked down her cheeks.

It wasn't long before she heard her door open and the familiar heavy footsteps of her father, Ben, walking into the kitchen. He didn't say anything as he sat down on the floor next to her and held her hand in his own.

Lily's tears fell harder as she buried her head in his shoulder. Sobs racked her body as she let go.

Her dad wrapped his arm around her shoulder and just held on, letting her know someone was there.

When her sobs finally stopped, he asked, "Do you want to talk about it?"

"There's not much to say."

"Say it anyway," he said gently.

"It's Chase. He's married."

Her dad glanced down at her. "I thought his wife passed away."

Lily let out a humorless laugh. "Yeah, I thought so, too. But I saw her today. She was at his house and they were... close."

"Wow. That's a lot to take in," Ben said softly.

"Need some wine?" she offered.

He held up the empty bottle that was sitting near her. "I think I'll pass."

"Your loss," she said with a halfhearted shrug.

Her phone started ringing again. Lily glanced at it and hit ignore.

"You don't want to talk to him?" Ben asked.

"Never again," she said.

Ben nodded. "I can see that. Probably better not to talk until you're sober anyway."

She jerked upright. "Am I drunk?"

"Can you feel your lips?"

Lily prodded at her mouth and shook her head.

"Yep. You're definitely drunk," he confirmed. "We should probably get some water in you and get you to bed." Her dad helped her to her feet and started to guide her toward the stairs.

"Wait," she cried, trying to reach for her phone again. "I need to call Evan."

"I'll do it," her dad assured her. He picked up her phone and put it in his pocket. "Let's go."

Before Lily knew what was happening, her father was tucking her into bed and handing her a glass of water.

"Evan?" she asked as she placed the glass on her nightstand.

"I'm calling now," Ben said. He fiddled with her phone and soon enough he was talking. Then he put the phone to her ear. "Tell your son goodnight."

"Evan?"

"Hi, Mom. Grandpa says you aren't feeling too good. Are you all right?"

"I'll be fine," she slurred and then winced when she heard it. She'd never been drunk in front of her son before. "I love you."

"I love you, too."

"Goodnight, Ev."

"Night, Mom."

Her dad took the phone from her and talked to Evan a little longer before ending the call.

"I didn't ask him what they did today," she said, sounding pitiful to her own ears.

"They went ice skating on the top of the mountain," Ben said. "He said Melissa skated with him and it was okay, but he'd have rather just stayed home and built a snowman."

"That sounds like my boy."

Ben put the water in her hand and ordered, "Drink."

Lily did as she was told. The last thing she remembered before she passed out was her dad taking the glass out of her hand and telling her he'd be right back.

CHASE WAS WORRIED. Lily hadn't shown up for dinner, and after a few unanswered phone calls, he was finally worried enough that he got into his car and drove over to her house. Her car was in the driveway and the porch light was on, making him certain she was home.

He bounded up to the door and knocked.

Only it wasn't Lily who answered, it was her father.

"Chase," her father said, his tone ice cold.

What was that about? Had Chase done something wrong? "Uh, hey, Ben. I'm looking for Lily. Is she home?"

"She's here, but she's sick in bed. I've turned her phone off for the evening."

"She's sick? With what? Is there anything I can do? Soup or—"

"I've got it under control, Chase. Go home." His eyes narrowed, and Chase was certain he saw hatred staring back at him. "To your wife." Then the door slammed in his face and the porch light went off, leaving him in the dark.

"Oh, hell," Chase muttered and walked back to his car with his head hung low. Somehow, someone had seen Hilary and had jumped to the wrong conclusion. And it was clear that Lily knew. His gut ached. It took all of his energy to not break in to her house and run upstairs to explain. Except he was fairly certain Ben Whitley would not appreciate that at all. There was nothing to do but wait until Chase saw her in the morning to explain his wife's twin.

~

LILY WOKE to a splitting headache and a churning stomach. She grabbed her head with both hands and rolled over, trying to block out the world. What in the hell had she done the night before? When she was fairly positive that her head wasn't going to explode, she braved sitting up and squinted through the bright light of the morning sun.

It took her a moment to register that the light streaming in from outside meant that she was late for work. "Oh, no!" she cried and scrambled out of bed, only to have to run to the bathroom where she lost the contents of her stomach.

Miserable and ready to die, she crawled back to the bed and reached for her phone. There was a note attached to it that read, *I called Mrs. Pottson and told her you weren't going to make it in today. It's just as well as there's a storm coming. Drink plenty of water, eat some carbs, and take a pain killer. You'll probably feel better by midafternoon. Dad.*

Feeling like death, Lily sipped some of the water her dad had left her and crawled back into bed. Since he'd called her in sick, there was nothing left to do but sleep it off.

The dream was fuzzy at first, but then it suddenly came into sharp focus.

Her ex, Sean, was sitting on the edge of a hotel bed with his shirt unbuttoned and his hair mussed. He was watching a petite brunette as she slowly unzipped her skin-tight electric-blue dress.

"How long do you have?" the woman asked him.

"Long enough. Melissa has my son to occupy her now. She won't even notice I'm gone."

The woman walked over and straddled him. "How long until you have access to her trust fund?"

Sean chuckled. "You're worse than I am. Patience, angel. Patience."

She pouted. "I'm tired of being patient, Sean. I won't wait around in that crappy apartment for long."

He ran a finger along her neck and kissed her jaw before saying, "You know I'm good for it. As soon as we're married and I have direct access to her money, I'll get you your own condo overlooking the lake. Just trust me."

The woman narrowed her eyes, studying him. "Are you trustworthy?"

Sean threw his head back and laughed. "No."

CHAPTER TWENTY-SIX

*C*hase was in no mood to be messed with. Lily hadn't come into work. There was a storm brewing, and the power kept flickering on and off. That meant there was no way he was going to get the orders out that day, much less stock up for the rest that were due before Christmas.

"Chase?" Ilsa called as she poked her head into the back. "We're closing early today. This storm is just moving in too fast."

"Okay. I need to clean up before I can go," he said.

"You know the drill. Lock up when you're done."

"Ilsa?" he asked.

"Yeah?"

"Have you heard from Lily today?"

She shook her head. "Sorry. Her dad just said she wasn't feeling well. She hasn't called you?"

"Nope."

"I'm sure she's just sleeping. She'll call when she's feeling a little better."

Chase doubted it, but he nodded and went back to cleaning his workstation.

About twenty minutes after Ilsa left, the shop phone rang. Chase contemplated ignoring it, but when it didn't stop, he finally picked it up. "Love Potions."

"Chase?" the young voice on the other end asked.

"Evan? Is that you?"

"Yes. Is my mom there?"

Chase frowned. "No. She called in sick today. What's wrong?"

"I can't get her on the phone and I…" He paused as if he didn't know what to say.

"What is it, Evan? I'll run over there and get a message to her. I'm getting ready to leave anyway."

"It's my dad and Melissa. She left late last night. And when my dad woke up this morning and realized she wasn't here, he got really mad and broke a lot of things. Then he told me to call my mom to come get me because he didn't have time to deal with it. After that, he left."

Chase's heart started to pound against his breastbone. "Where are you? Are you safe? Did your dad hurt you?"

"I'm at the condo he brought us to, and I'm safe, but there's really not much food here. They were getting takeout. He didn't hurt me. Not really."

"Not really? What does that mean?" Chase wanted to start throwing things himself, but he refrained. There was no point in trashing Mrs. Pottson's store.

"I stepped on a broken plate and cut my foot, but I'm all right. It stopped bleeding after I wrapped it in a washcloth."

Oh, for the love of everything holy. Chase hated Evan's father with a passion. "Okay, Evan, I need you to do something for me. Can you find something there with the address? Like a piece of mail or a business card?"

"Give me a second." There was rustling on the other end of the line, and when Evan spoke again, he said, "I found an invoice on the counter."

"Good. Read me the address."

Evan rattled off the address in South Lake Tahoe. Chase recognized the complex. He'd stayed there before. It wasn't exactly a vacation home. More like a timeshare. "Perfect. I'm on my way. I'll be there in a few hours. Hold tight, okay?"

"Will you call my mom?"

"Of course, buddy. Don't worry about a thing. We'll have you home soon."

Evan let out a relieved breath. "Okay. Thank you."

Chase jotted down the number that had come up on caller ID and hurried out of the store. The moment he stepped outside his anxiety ratcheted up to an alarming level. The storm was worse than he'd thought. He quickly checked his storm tracker and found out it was coming in from the west. If the pass wasn't closed yet, it would be soon. There was no time to do anything other than get on the road.

As he jumped into his SUV, he tried to call Lily. It went straight to voice mail. He'd have called Ben, Lily's father, but he didn't have his number. His next tries were Zach and Rex, but the calls didn't even go through. His phone just beeped. He figured the cell towers must have gone down.

He had a choice to make. Get on the road and to Evan as soon as possible, or stop at Lily's and risk the pass closing. But before he had to make that decision, he spotted Hilary coming out of a gas station. He swerved into the station and pulled up to her car.

"There's been an emergency," he told her. "I need a favor."

"Anything," she said. "As long as it doesn't include driving in this. I just ran down to stock up on eggs and snack food before I hole up next to the fireplace."

He winced and explained what he needed.

"I'm on it," she said solemnly. "Go. That kid needs you."

"Thank you." Chase pointed the car toward the freeway and prayed he had enough time to outrun the storm.

LILY PACED HER KITCHEN. After dreamwalking her ex, she'd woken with a start and with an ache in the pit of her stomach. Or had it been a vision? The scene had been really specific. Lily supposed either were a possibility. She was grateful the hangover had subsided, but now she was nauseated by Sean's actions.

If that wasn't enough, she'd also woken with an uneasy feeling that something was very wrong. Something besides the fact that Sean was still a cheating A-hole who was only marrying Melissa for her money. She clutched her phone, waiting for a signal. The storm had apparently knocked out the cell towers and the internet provider, and her only forms of communication had been rendered useless.

Lily hated feeling isolated and considered heading over to Ilsa's, but when she glanced outside, the snow had really started to fall and she didn't want to risk getting caught in the storm, especially when her phone wasn't working.

She was still pacing ten minutes later when a knock sounded on her door. Lily rushed to open it and nearly slammed it in the face of the woman standing on her porch.

But before she could make a move, the tall blonde said, "Chase sent me. He's on his way to get Evan."

"Evan?" Lily echoed as her stomach churned. "Chase is getting Evan? Why?"

The woman shivered and wrapped her arms around herself. "Evan called the store. He said he couldn't get ahold of you, so he tried there. He told Chase he's been left alone. That his dad told him to have you come get him."

Lily heard the words but was having trouble comprehending anything. Her ears were buzzing, and her eyes wouldn't focus. She wondered if this was what it meant when someone froze under pressure.

"Lily? Can I come in?" the woman asked.

"What? Oh. Yeah, I guess." She opened the door for her, and when she closed it, Lily said, "It's Heather, right?"

The woman spun around, her eyes wide with shock. "Heather? No. Heather was my sister. I'm Hilary, Chase's sister-in-law."

Lily stared at her, dumbfounded for the second time in a few short minutes. "You're not his wife?"

Hilary choked a little before she shook her head. "My sister passed away."

"Right. I…" Lily squeezed her eyes shut and shook her head. "Sorry. I must've been confused. Can we get back to my son? You said he's alone. Where?"

Hilary took a seat on Lily's couch. "He's at the condo. I got the impression he's shook up but okay. Chase said he'd call as soon as the lines are up and running."

Lily unlocked her phone and tried Chase. Nothing. Then she tried Sean with the same result. There was no success with the landline number Melissa had given her either, and Lily flopped down onto the couch next to Hilary when she failed to reach anyone.

They were both quiet for a while until Lily turned to her and asked, "Are you having an affair with Chase?"

"No," she said, sounding exhausted.

"Then why were you kissing him yesterday?" None of this mattered in light of what was happening with her son, but Lily needed something to distract herself before she lost her mind with worry.

"It's a long story, but the short version is that I was hoping he'd be my baby daddy."

Lily turned to stare at her, trying to decide if she was serious. "Your baby daddy?"

Hilary covered her eyes with her hand and nodded. "Turns out I'm pregnant, and the father bailed. Chase is the most responsible person I know. Who else would I ask to help me raise my kid?"

"He is pretty great," Lily agreed. "What did he say?"

"He told me I'm nuts, that we'd never be anything more than brother- and sister-in-law, but that he'd be there for me and my baby, no matter what."

"That sounds like Chase," Lily said as she plucked at the edges of a throw pillow.

"He really cares about you. You know that, right?" Hilary said.

Lily nodded. She did know that. He also cared about her kid. Who else would drop everything to drive through a storm to pick up someone else's kid without even being asked? "He'll be okay, won't he?"

"Evan? Sure. He's safe in a condo. He knew who to call for help. I'm sure everything will be just fine."

"And Chase? He'll make it okay, right?" Lily knew the other woman didn't have the answers, but she still had to ask. She needed someone to reassure her.

"Chase will definitely be fine," she said and reached over to squeeze Lily's hand.

Lily glanced at her. "Congratulations on the baby."

"Thanks. I'm terrified."

"I was, too. Still am. You'll get used to it."

Hilary chuckled. "That's reassuring."

"That's parenthood." Lily glanced at her phone, and despite no evidence of a signal, she tried again to call Evan. It rang once, and then he picked up.

"Hello?" he said.

"Oh, thank the gods. Evan, are you okay?"

"Mom?"

The reception crackled, and Lily just started talking. "Chase is on his way, baby. He'll be there as soon as possible. Everything is going to be just fine, okay?"

The crackling stopped and a second later, Lily heard that dreaded beeping that indicated a dropped call. She immediately tried him again, but nothing went through. Still, she'd heard his voice and Chase was on his way. Evan was going to be okay, and as soon as Lily laid eyes on him, she would be too.

CHAPTER TWENTY-SEVEN

The normal two-hour drive to Lake Tahoe took Chase just over five hours in the storm. He'd followed a snow plow almost the entire way, and by the time he made it to the address that Evan had given him, it was dark outside. As soon as he parked, he pulled his phone out and called the number Evan had given him.

There was no answer, despite there being service.

Chase jumped out of the SUV and jogged around, checking unit numbers until he found the one he was looking for. The lights were off, and when he pounded on the door, there was no answer.

Dread coiled in his stomach. Where was Evan? Had his father come back and taken him somewhere? Did he tell Lily? What was Chase going to tell her? He pounded harder and yelled, "Evan?"

The door across the hall opened, and a young woman in jeans and an oversized sweater appeared. "If you're looking for the boy who was here, child services came for him a few hours ago."

"Child services?" he asked. "Why?"

She eyed him with suspicion. "Because of the altercation. His dad went into a crazy rage, throwing stuff. I was worried the kid was in danger."

Chase closed his eyes and took a deep breath. "Can I have the number you called?"

"Why?"

"Because I'm here to take him home to his mother," Chase said, trying to be patient. She had, after all, been looking out for Evan. "Evan called us earlier today to tell us what happened with his dad. I came as soon as we heard."

"Who are you?" she asked.

"A family friend." His patience was waning.

"Where's his mother?"

"At home, riding out the storm. Listen, Ms...."

"Carson."

"Ms. Carson, I truly appreciate your concern for Evan. His mother is worried sick about him, and the sooner I find him the sooner I can help get him home to her. She would be here if there was any possible way, but with the storm, she couldn't just jump in her car and make the trip. So if you could just give me the number, I'd be very appreciative."

"His mother isn't the one who was staying here with him, was she?"

"No. That was his soon-to-be stepmother. But it seems those plans may have gone off the rails."

She nodded, closed the door, and reappeared with a phone number a few seconds later. "Good luck, man. It sounds like you've walked into a giant mess."

"Thanks," he said, taking the number and ignoring the rest. He didn't need her judgment.

Getting through to child services and figuring out where

they'd taken Evan felt like it took longer than it had to get to Lake Tahoe. No one wanted to give a nonrelative information. It wasn't until the cell towers were restored in Christmas Grove and they got Lily on the phone that he was finally given access to Evan.

Chase walked up to the temporary foster care center and met one of the social workers outside.

"Mr. Garland?" the woman asked, holding her hand out to him.

"Yes. Is Evan ready to go?"

She nodded. "Sorry about the runaround. These things can be very tricky when there's a question if the child is in danger. I'm sure you understand."

"Yeah. I do. But it's been a really long day, and Evan's mother is anxious to get him home. So if we could just get on the road, I'd really appreciate it."

"Of course." She tapped in a message on her phone.

A moment later, Evan ran out of the house with a backpack slung over his arm and hurled himself into Chase's arms.

"Hey, buddy," Chase soothed as he clutched the boy to his chest. "Everything is going to be just fine now."

"I want to go home," Evan said through his tears.

"I know. We're going to go straight there. Your mom can't wait to see you."

Evan nodded. "They let me Facetime her."

Chase lifted his gaze to the social worker and mouthed, *Thank you.*

You're welcome, she mouthed back and then slipped back inside.

Chase took Evan by the hand and led him to his SUV. "Are you hungry?"

"Starving."

"Me, too. How do you feel about fast food?" Chase asked.

Evan beamed. "Can we get French fries?"

"As many as you'd like."

⁓

LILY WAITED UP HALF the night until Chase finally parked in her driveway. As soon as she saw the headlights, Lily ran out the door and scooped Evan into her arms.

He let out a cry and clung to her.

Neither said anything. They just held on. After a while she said, "That's never going to happen again."

He pulled back slightly. "I don't have to go with dad again?"

"Not if I have anything to say about it." Lily had already been on the phone with her lawyer, and she was pretty adamant that she'd be able to get Lily full custody. As frustrated as Lily was that the condo neighbor had involved child services, making it harder for them to get Evan home, it had created a record of events. Lily's lawyer said that the violent nature of Sean's behavior, combined with the abandonment, would be more than enough for Lily to win full custody. She'd already filed for an emergency injunction so that Sean couldn't see him until the next court hearing.

"Good. I don't ever want to go back with him."

"I know, buddy. You won't have to." She held him close and then looked up at Chase. He was standing a few feet away with his hands in his pockets, just watching them. When she released Evan from the hug, she kept hold of one of his hands and then held out the other to Chase. "Let's go inside."

Chase gave her a small smile, took her hand, and together all three of them walked into her house.

Once they had Evan safely in his bed, Lily turned to Chase. "I'm sorry."

"For what?" he asked, furrowing his brow.

"For not stopping to find out what was happening with Hilary. I saw her kiss you and jumped to all kinds of wrong conclusions."

Chase groaned and ran a hand down his face. "I can imagine it was a shock to see her. It's okay. I completely understand why you came to the wrong conclusions."

"It still wasn't fair of me," she said. "I have no reason not to trust you. I should have at least taken your call."

"Speaking of trust, there's something I need to tell you about Hilary."

Lily stiffened, her defenses sliding back into place. Had something happened with Hilary? Her stomach ached with dread. "What is it?"

"She's pregnant," he blurted then backtracked. "It's not mine. I mean, there's no possible way it could be mine. I would never, *ever* go there with her. That's not... Oh, hell."

Lily smirked. "You're cute when you're nervous. I already knew. She told me everything."

"Right. Okay. Well, she came to me because she needs someone stable in her life, and I promised I'd help her however I could with my niece or nephew. I just wanted you to know because I'm in this with you, and if this kid is going to be in my life, that's going to affect you and Evan. Are you okay with that?"

"With you being a presence in a kids life?" Lily truly had no issue with that, but she wasn't sure what to make of Hilary. "Of course, I'm fine with that. He or she will be very lucky to have you in their corner. But what does that mean for us and Hilary? What kind of support do you plan to give her?"

"She's set financially. It's the emotional support she'll need. She doesn't really have any family left, so this is overwhelming for her. I told her she could stay at my place until she finds her own. Is that going to be a problem?"

"No. I don't think so." It was a lot to take in, but Lily had been a single mom long enough to know just how hard it could be. She'd just met Hilary, but she liked her and hoped they'd become friends.

"Let's make a deal," Chase said. "How about we promise to always hear each other out, no matter what else is going on?"

"Deal," Lily said. She pressed up onto her tiptoes and gave him the kiss she'd been dying to give him ever since she'd laid eyes on him in her driveway. "You were my hero today."

He chuckled. "I'm not a hero. I'm just a guy who cares an awful lot about you and Evan."

Lily sobered. "You put us ahead of everything, including your own safety. That's... everything to me. I hope you know just how much I appreciate you." She shook her head. "No, make that how much I *love* you."

His lips curved up into a slow smile. "I love you, too, Lily Paddington."

"That's good," she whispered as she started to tug him toward the stairs.

Chase cast a glance toward the second floor and then back at her. "Are you inviting me upstairs?"

She grinned. "I'm inviting you to stay the night. What's it going to be, Mr. Garland? My bedroom or are you headed home?"

"Is that a real choice?" he asked with a chuckle.

She shrugged a shoulder. "Some guys spook easily."

"Not me." He wrapped his hand around hers and headed for the stairs. "Given the chance, I'll stay here every night."

"Even though you're a trust-fund baby?"

He frowned at her. "Who told you that?"

"Sean. He seemed to think I was with you for your money."

"Are you?" Chase asked with one raised eyebrow.

"No," she said with a chuckle. "I have no idea if it's true. And I really don't care."

He nodded. "Seems like your ex did an awful lot of digging around in our lives."

Lily sighed. "He did know stuff he shouldn't."

Chase just shrugged. "It's true. I have a trust fund. A small one. Mostly it gets used for the Christmas Grove animal rescue."

"Really? Does that give you access to puppies that need to be adopted?" She'd been reconsidering her stance on the puppy situation. She'd seen how much joy Zach's dog brought Evan, and with everything that had gone on, she just wanted Evan to have more love in his life. A puppy would definitely be more work, but she was tired of always having to say no. They'd make it work. Besides, Evan wasn't the only one who wanted a dog around. She'd wasn't immune to their big puppy-dog eyes. And if Chase could make it easier for them to find one, then all the better.

"I thought you were anti-puppy for Christmas," he said.

"A girl has a right to change her mind."

He grinned. "Okay, sure. What kind are you looking for?"

"One for Evan. Like a Lab or golden retriever. Something gentle but indestructible."

He nodded. "I'll see what I can do."

"Okay," she said. "Ready for bed?"

"More than ready." Chase held onto her hand and led her up the stairs.

~

THREE DAYS LATER, Lily woke to the sounds of a puppy stamping his paws at the end of her bed. She opened one eye and spotted her son sneaking toward them. He had a tray holding a plate of pancakes and a couple of mugs.

Lily remained silent as she watched him place their breakfast on the nightstand but then bolted upright the moment he jumped on the bed, right between her and Chase. The six-month-old golden retriever they'd just adopted followed him onto the bed, creating mayhem.

"Got you!" Lily cried, just as Evan yelled, "Merry Christmas!"

Chase groaned his displeasure as the puppy licked his face. There was no sleeping through their antics. "It's way too early for this," he complained.

"But Santa was here," Evan said, snuggling in next to Lily, who'd wrapped her arm around his shoulders. His dog, Jingles, turned his focus to Evan and started demanding attention until Evan scratched his ears.

"Santa isn't real," Chase grumbled.

Lily let out a loud gasp. "How dare you?" she teased. "We're believers in this house. So get on board, or we might have to trade you in for someone with a little more cheer."

Chase rolled onto his back and peered up at her. "You're not trading anyone in."

It had only been a few days since they'd worked everything out, but she had to admit he was right. Chase had been with them almost nonstop, and to Lily's amazement, Chase's integration into their lives had been seamless.

Evan loved him. And he loved Evan. They were like two

peas in a pod when they were working on something together. Lily had no doubt Chase would do anything for her son. In fact, if they ever got married, she figured Chase would adopt him.

Now that Sean had signed away his rights, that would be possible. It had only been two days after Evan had returned home when Lily got word that Sean had terminated his parental rights. It turned out that Melissa had been his meal ticket and without her, he didn't even have money to pay his lawyer. With the threat of back child support looming over him, he'd cut a deal to sever ties. Lily's lawyer advised that she could be leaving money on the table, but Lily didn't care. All she wanted was for Evan to never have to deal with his deadbeat dad again.

"I made you breakfast," Evan said.

Lily glanced at her tray and smiled when she spotted pancakes. "Thank you. That was very sweet of you."

Evan crawled off the bed and Jingles followed him. "Go ahead and eat so we can get Christmas started."

Lily frowned at him. They'd already exchanged presents before he left on his abbreviated trip to Lake Tahoe. What more could there be? She glanced over at Chase, who was busy digging into his pancakes and acting like he hadn't heard a thing. Lily eyed them both, trying to figure it out, but then she got a whiff of Chase's coffee.

She gave up and dug into her breakfast.

When they were done eating, Evan coaxed them out of bed and led them downstairs where there were four presents. One for each of them, including the puppy. Jingles curled up into the dog bed and stared at them as if he was just as curious as they were.

Lily turned to Chase. "Did you do this?"

"I'm pretty sure the tag says they're from Santa," he said, rocking back on his heels.

"Okay, *Santa*," she said, rolling her eyes.

He just laughed. "I swear it wasn't me."

There was something in his tone that indicated he was telling the truth. Lily glanced at her son, wondering if he'd put this together, but the packages were far too professional. If they'd been left to Evan, they'd have been wrapped in brown paper bags.

Lily picked up the gifts and handed them out. "Who's first?"

Evan raised his hand. "Me!"

Chase and Lily watched as he carefully unwrapped his gift and then let out a squeal when he spotted the train that went perfectly with the set that Chase had gotten him. "I love it!" he cried and ran to give Chase a hug.

"I swear, I didn't do this," Chase whispered to Lily.

"You can keep saying that, but no one believes you," Lily teased.

"Okay, but you're the one who still believes Santa's real."

Lily chuckled. "Fair enough." She turned her attention to Evan again. "Help Jingles with his gift."

Evan tore into the package and found a chew toy that Jingles promptly stole from him.

Then it was Lily's turn. She opened her gift and was speechless as she pulled the art deco watch out of the box. It was exactly like the one her mother used to wear. The one she'd been looking for as long as she could remember. "Did my dad tell you this was what I wanted?" she asked Chase.

He shook his head. "I told you already, this wasn't me."

"Okay, whatever you say. Open yours," she ordered.

Chase tore through the paper and then was speechless. His

gift was a pair of antique salt and pepper shakers. They were silver and in the shape of a witch's hat and broom.

"Chase?" Lily asked. "Do those mean something to you?"

He nodded. "They are just like the ones my grandmother had. The grandmother who taught me to love baking and encouraged me to be a chocolatier."

As they sat there staring at each other, a fire magically appeared in her fireplace, and Lily was certain she heard the faint sound of *Ho, ho, ho, Merry Christmas* off in the distance.

"Did you hear that?" Evan asked.

Both Lily and Chase nodded. And when they turned to look at the cookies they'd left for Santa, the only thing left on the tray was a handwritten note that read, *Enjoy each other. I'll be back next year with more magic. Love, S.*

CHAPTER TWENTY-EIGHT

ELEVEN MONTHS LATER

*O*livia Mann stood in the kitchen of her new inn, nearly having a panic attack. Her head chef had just dropped the news three days ago that she'd fractured her leg and was out of commission for the next three months.

If this had happened at any other time, she'd have just closed the kitchen. But this December Olivia had an inn full of actors and actresses who would be in residence. It was in the contract that the inn would feed them three times a day while they filmed a holiday special about her town, Christmas Grove. She couldn't cancel, and she couldn't let them down. This contract was the thing that would help her make it into the black her first year in business.

"Cara," she said, clutching her phone as she talked to her longtime friend who also happened to be a headhunter. "Isn't there anyone who's willing to come to Christmas Grove and have a chance to work with celebrities?"

The woman on the other end of the phone let out a laugh. "Do you really think celebrities are a selling point for this job?"

"Aren't they?" Olivia asked. Didn't most people want to meet celebrities?

"No, not at all. Celebrities are demanding and far more likely to complain. No chef wants that, and certainly not for a temporary gig up in the mountains. I'm sorry, Olivia. If it were a full-time position, I think we'd have a better shot, but finding someone with the culinary skills you require for a short-term gig is proving to be tough. No one is interested."

"Okay." Olivia leaned against the wall and pressed her hand to her forehead. "We'll figure something out. We always do. I bet I can drum someone up with my contacts." It was a lie. Olivia had already called everyone she knew in the industry to inquire about a temporary chef, and either everyone was already employed, or they weren't willing to relocate for three months, despite the fact that room and board was included.

"Uh, Olivia?" Cara said. "There is one option."

"No," Olivia said automatically. "Not him."

"I don't think you have a choice," her friend said.

"I told you—"

The door to the kitchen swung open, and a tall, broad-shouldered man with sandy blond hair walked in wearing his chef's whites.

Declan McCabe. The one man Olivia had hoped to never see again.

He swept his gaze over her and gave her a mocking smile. "I hear you need someone to rescue you."

"I don't need anyone to rescue me, and certainly not *you*," she shot back.

"Oh, good," Cara said into the phone. "I see he's there already. Good luck!"

"Cara!" Olivia cried, but it was too late. Her friend had already ended the call. She locked the screen in disgust and then turned her attention to the arrogant man standing in front of her. "I didn't hire you."

He pursed his lips and glanced around. "It sure looks like you did. I have a contract."

Olivia swallowed a groan. Damn that Cara. This is what she deserved for trusting her friend to hire someone competent.

Except Declan McCabe was more than competent, so Cara had actually done her job. It was just that Olivia had asked her to hire *anyone* but him. "Fine. You have a contract. But let's just keep this professional, shall we?"

Declan moved in until he was just inches away from Olivia. Then he lowered his voice and asked, "What's wrong, Olivia? Are you afraid your staff is going to find out you slept with your head chef?"

"Temporary head chef. And there's no reason for anyone to know our private business. Let's just... keep it professional."

Declan swept his smoldering gaze over her, making her body heat from the inside as he said, "I will if you will."

Olivia shuddered, and then without a word, she stalked out of his kitchen.

DEANNA'S BOOK LIST

Witches of Keating Hollow:
Soul of the Witch
Heart of the Witch
Spirit of the Witch
Dreams of the Witch
Courage of the Witch
Love of the Witch
Power of the Witch
Essence of the Witch
Muse of the Witch
Vision of the Witch
Waking of the Witch
Honor of the Witch

Witches of Christmas Grove:
A Witch For Mr. Holiday
A Witch For Mr. Christmas
A Witch For Mr. Winter
A Witch For Mr. Mistletoe

Premonition Pointe Novels:

Witching For Grace

Witching For Hope

Witching For Joy

Witching For Clarity

Witching For Moxie

Witching For Kismet

Miss Matched Midlife Dating Agency:

Star-crossed Witch

Honor-bound Witch

Outmatched Witch

Jade Calhoun Novels:

Haunted on Bourbon Street

Witches of Bourbon Street

Demons of Bourbon Street

Angels of Bourbon Street

Shadows of Bourbon Street

Incubus of Bourbon Street

Bewitched on Bourbon Street

Hexed on Bourbon Street

Dragons of Bourbon Street

Pyper Rayne Novels:

Spirits, Stilettos, and a Silver Bustier

Spirits, Rock Stars, and a Midnight Chocolate Bar

Spirits, Beignets, and a Bayou Biker Gang

Spirits, Diamonds, and a Drive-thru Daiquiri Stand

Spirits, Spells, and Wedding Bells

Ida May Chronicles:

Witched To Death
Witch, Please
Stop Your Witchin'

Crescent City Fae Novels:
Influential Magic
Irresistible Magic
Intoxicating Magic

Last Witch Standing:
Bewitched by Moonlight
Soulless at Sunset
Bloodlust By Midnight
Bitten At Daybreak

Witch Island Brides:
The Wolf's New Year Bride
The Vampire's Last Dance
The Warlock's Enchanted Kiss
The Shifter's First Bite

Destiny Novels:
Defining Destiny
Accepting Fate

Wolves of the Rising Sun:
Jace
Aiden
Luc
Craved
Silas
Darien

Wren

Black Bear Outlaws:
Cyrus
Chase
Cole

Bayou Springs Alien Mail Order Brides:
Zeke
Gunn
Echo

ABOUT THE AUTHOR

New York Times and USA Today bestselling author, Deanna Chase, is a native Californian, transplanted to the slower paced lifestyle of southeastern Louisiana. When she isn't writing, she is often goofing off with her husband in New Orleans or playing with her two shih tzu dogs. For more information and updates on newest releases visit her website at deannachase.com.

Made in United States
North Haven, CT
24 February 2023